Nothing but the Truth

Nothing but the Truth

Ulla Bolinder

Translated from the Swedish by
Eric Swanson
in collaboration with the author

Originally published in Sweden as
Ingenting annat än sanningen
by BoD 2020
© Ulla Bolinder 2020
English Translation © Eric Swanson 2021
Cover: Ulla Bolinder
Cover photos: Pixabay
Publisher: BoD – Books on Demand, Stockholm, Sweden
Print: BoD – Books on Demand, Norderstedt, Germany
ISBN: 978-91-7851-818-0

*What happened to you was not your fault.
It was not something you asked for, it was not
something you deserved.
What happened to you was not fair. Trauma is not
your fault, but healing is your responsibility.*
Brianna Wiest

Love is your freedom, born of awareness.
Ivan Rados

PART ONE

The door is open now. I am not shut-in anymore. Several times every day a great sorrow wells up in me and makes me start crying. I cry when I wake up, I cry when I wash myself, I cry when I put on clean underwear, I cry when I exert myself physically, I cry when I shower, I cry when I go to bed and curl up under the covers, I cry when I see a police car on the street.

Sometimes, when I have to control myself because there are other people around, I become angry instead. *I will kill you,* I think. *You are going to die.*

Sometimes I don't feel sad at all and think that the grief has disappeared and won't come back. But it does.

What is it due to, and where was it before? Has it always been there, although I didn't know about it, or is it new? Does it have to do with the rape? Am I not done with it yet, although I thought so?

I don't need to go through in my mind what happened anymore, and I don't need to talk about it, and I don't need to get understanding and consolation from other people. Or do I deceive myself when I think like that?

In a book about rape, I read:

The study makes apparent that what these women experienced is not a story that has an ending. For some of the women it is an ongoing trauma in which new problems are piled upon the burden they already bear. For several of the women the situation at the time of the interview was stable; but both this study and those of others show how fragile this stability is. The limitations of crisis theory become more apparent; what these women experienced was not something they could come to terms with and put behind them once and for all as one of life´s ordinary experiences.

But it feels so distant now, and I don't understand what the point would be to go into it again. Or would it be good? Should I tell Göran after all? He knows it has happened, but he doesn't know in what way or how bad it was.

The distance between us has become greater again, although I felt before that we were close. Would it decrease if I told him about the rape and he told me about the car accident he has been involved in? He must also bear a great grief that he may need to talk about. If he doesn't want to, I accept it. Then I have shown that I am able and prepared anyway. The thought almost paralyzes me, but I have to try, so that we at least get a chance to move on.

Göran has always been so indistinct to me, and I don't want it to be like that anymore. He is as quiet and withdrawn as I am, so it's difficult to form an opinion about him. But to me, he is like Russian Folk Song sounds when Arne Lamberth plays it on the trumpet. That may not be true, but that's how I feel.

I have thought about him so much, longed so much and fantasized so much. He is the only one I trust, and the only one I know who might be able to cope with me. He is strong and considerate and never intrusive. That he came to my home that time when Bernt was on a course and I was sick, wasn't like him at all. I didn't know how to interpret it and was confused.

Now it no longer matters what it meant. Now I will find out who he is and what he feels and wants. It won't be easy, but I am tired of walking around and just guessing. I want to *know*. And it feels like it's my fault that we haven't become closer even though we have worked together for so long. When he has approached me, I have rejected him, and I don't want to do that anymore. It's different now that I am no longer closed, but he doesn't know, and that's why I have to take the initiative and show him what I want.

Mamma doesn't call so often anymore. Now that I have exposed her, and she notices that I no longer let her take advantage of me, she doesn't get in touch. If it was me she was interested in, she would call, but she doesn't, because she is only interested in herself.

Before I had really felt what she was doing to me, and always has, and how sorry I was that she didn't care about me, I couldn't reject her. Instead, I dodged out of it and made excuses to avoid protesting seriously. I thought it was my duty to always be accommodating, no matter how uninterested I was in what she had to say. The mistake I made was that I really tried to listen, and that I thought it was just me she wanted to have contact with.

Now I know that when she calls, I could just as well put down the receiver and start washing up the dishes while she is talking. She is so in her own world that she wouldn't notice if I wasn't there. She will never understand what she has done, and still would do, if she only had the opportunity.

But she gets no more opportunities. She can complain as much as she wants that I never call, and never come and visit her, and never listen to her, because she can't control me, and now her power over me is gone.

Before Petra met her boyfriend and moved to Germany, I accompanied her out and danced sometimes. It was mostly for her sake, to keep her company, and not because I am so fond of dancing. And the guys I didn't care about. I was together with Bernt, and it never crossed my mind to be unfaithful.

Or did I deceive myself even then? Did I go out with Petra because I felt that Bernt's and my relationship wasn't good, and I was hoping to meet a better guy? I had nothing to compare with and thought that what Bernt and I had was normal. But it wasn't.

Could I tell Göran how I felt about Bernt without feeling ashamed? Could I tell him that I agreed to sex even though I didn't want to? That I didn't react negatively when he used vulgar and derogatory words about my body? That I let him insert a cucumber in me because he wanted me to experience "a real fucking bull"? Could I tell him how stupid I was who didn't feel humiliated?

I told Petra, and when she heard about the

cucumber, she said:

"Yes, he probably has got bad self-confidence because you are never turned on by him. Of course, he must notice that. So maybe he was trying to compensate you."

I don't remember what I answered, but if that were the case, you can almost feel sorry for him.

It was just as much my fault that we weren't well. I know that. I felt no confidence in him and never told him what I thought about things that were important to me. I felt superior to him and thought he was immature and ridiculous. I didn't realize that I was as immature myself, but in a different way.

I am glad it ended and that we won't meet anymore. I am glad I have learned what's right and what's wrong. But I have no experience of the right thing. For example, how much should you tell about yourself in a good relationship? You can't tell another person just everything. But how much is it normal to keep to oneself?

I don't know, and that's why I think of it now when I consider confiding in Göran. I also want to test him, so that I can know for sure what kind of person he is. It may be lousy to have that ulterior motive, but as long as I don't know, I can't let go.

No one but the police have asked me to tell about the rape, and it was only because it was their job to find out what had happened. No one has asked and wanted to know for *my* sake. Not mamma, not Bernt, not Bernt's parents…

I cry when I think about it. *Nobody wants to know, nobody wants to know, why is nobody wanting to know, why is nobody helping me?*

I had no one to tell. I had nowhere to go. There was no one to turn to and no one I thought would understand. I didn't know I was sorry for that. But it must mean that no one cared about me.

Does Göran care about me? I don't need help any longer, but does he care about me? That's what I am going to find out now.

I don't want to lie to Göran. If I am going to tell him about the rape, I want to tell the truth.

How do I accomplish that?

I have to admit to myself what I was lying about and be absolutely clear about it in advance, so that I can avoid getting into revealing details. I won't tell him the whole truth.

How could the police think that what I first told them took a whole hour? Why was no one reacting and thinking it was strange?

I said that what happened started at half past ten, which meant that it must have lasted for almost an hour. But when I answered what time it was, I knew the time wasn't right. After the cinema, I had also been standing on Västgötaspången and looked down at the water in Fyrisån, and I had walked around in the centre, and I had been sitting on a bench and smoking. I didn't know what I was waiting for and hoped would happen, but I didn't hurry home. It wasn't true that I missed the bus as I told the police.

My watch had stopped, and I didn't know what

time it was. When I was asked about it on the street, I answered with what the dial showed, and that time I also told the police to avoid explaining. I thought it would seem like I had stayed in town because I was looking for company. In a way, it was true and that wouldn't have looked good for me, I thought.

– So, you had been to the cinema?

– Yes.

– In which cinema?

– Spegeln.

– Spegeln? But then the bus stop on Drottninggatan or Stora torget must be nearer at hand?

– Yes, but I just missed a bus, and I thought I could walk a bit while I waited for the next one and get on at some stop further ahead.

Before I went out on the street afterwards, I had been lying unconscious inside the yard for a while. At first, I thought I had been lying there for a long time, but now I know that if you faint and fall, you wake up again after just a few minutes.

Fainting is caused by too little blood reaching the brain. This can happen if you get up too fast, have stood still for too long, or have eaten too little. You can also faint from stress, pain, or fear. But as soon as you lie down, the normal distribution of blood in the body is restored and you wake up again.

And I hadn't become cold. When I came out on the street, I was still warm. I felt through the ankle socks that the sidewalk was cooling, and I was trembling all over, but I wasn't freezing. When I woke up, I must have got up again and gone straight out on the street, but I have no memory of it.

– I sat up. At first, I lay on the ground for a while, and then I know I got up, but I don't remember going out on the street. I don't know how I got there.

– You have a gap in your memory there?

– Yes.

– But you remember the rest? That you met that guy who helped you into Lucullus and…

– Yes.

Why didn't I get dressed first? And why didn't I take my bag with me when I left? Before I fainted, I had decided to get dressed and go home. Instead, I just went out from there and left everything behind. I must have been so shocked that I couldn't think properly. I didn't remember the bag until I was out on the street and had met the guy who helped me into the restaurant afterwards.

Some things I didn't tell the police, and some things I even lied about. I didn't tell them what I felt and did right after the cinema, and I lied that I had missed the bus. I didn't tell them that I judged how the guy who stopped me seemed to be, as if he could be a nice acquaintance. I lied about what time it was not to have to explain what I had done earlier. I lied when I said I was frightened when he threatened me with a gun, and I didn't tell them what I said to him when he did it. I didn't tell them what I said when I tried to persuade him to let me go, nor did I tell them that I was just threatening to scream instead of really doing it. I thought I had reacted abnormally and was ashamed.

The worst thing is that I lied about the time. The police were looking for witnesses who could have made observations on Vaksalagatan at half past ten, the newspaper said afterwards. At that time, I hadn't even got there, and there was nothing to see. Or was he already standing there waiting for a suitable victim? He could have been seen long in advance. So maybe it didn't matter that I lied. At least now it doesn't matter. In the end, he still got caught, and that had nothing to do with me.

PART TWO

Viola once said that she finds it strange that no girl has "laid hands" on Göran, who is so "young and handsome." I think so too. Does he have a girl-friend although we at work haven't been told? The fact that he lives alone and has never mentioned her doesn't necessarily mean that she doesn't exist.

No, I don't think she exists. If she did, he wouldn't keep it a secret. In his car, which I go in almost every day, I have never felt any foreign scents or seen any things she could have forgotten or left there. That I have considered it at all, is because I wanted to be absolutely sure there were no obstacles before I invited him to my home so as not to make a fool of myself.

But I have still postponed it. At work I have observed him and listened to him and tried to imagine him in a different situation, and in the car on the way home, I have sat and worked myself up at the thought of getting it said.

Finally, however, I was ready. I had thought out in advance what I was going to say, and I had decided to do it two days before, so yesterday when he had stopped the car in the parking lot at home, I took courage and asked.

"Would you like to come in with me on Friday and have dinner?" I said.

If he was surprised, he didn't show it.

"Yes, thank you," he said and smiled.

I got completely weak by the way he said it and by his voice and smile. At the same time as I felt relieved and happy, I was ready to cry.

"It's a deal then," I said and hurried out of the car.

Today I asked him if he likes pizza and red wine, and he said he does, so now I have been out and purchased what's needed. I bought a few different kinds of pizza so that he can choose the one he likes best. When it comes to wine, I chose one that I myself think is good.

Maybe we shouldn't drink wine considering how easily you can lose control when you are affected. I am excited enough without it. Just the thought of him makes my body react and want to have him.

When he is here, I am not going to think about sex but try to find out more about how he is. At work, we never talk about private things, and if I don't do anything about it, it will continue as now forever. Nothing will change, and it doesn't feel right. It's because I want to get to know him that I have invited him, and not because we are going to have sex. But my body doesn't get it and prepares to receive him as soon as I think of him.

What have I started? Why do I have to do this? How will it end?

I must do it because it was wrong of me not to show response when he approached me before. I rejected him even though I didn't want to. I wasn't open and couldn't receive what he was trying to give me. It must not end like that. I don't want it to be my fault that it didn't become more, if it could be. I must show him that I am able now.

To be on the safe side, I will start by listening, because I know I am good at that. I have listened all my life whether I have wanted to or not. But now I want to because it's *him*.

I also want something else because it's him, but I am not going to think about it if I can keep it away. I am always so aware that he is a *man,* and what that means we can do. With Bernt it didn't feel like this at all, but I wasn't in love with him, I suppose.

Am I in love with Göran? I think so, but I don't know. It mostly feels like I am physically attracted to him. Turned on by him, as Bernt would have said. Yes, I am, and that's what makes me extra nervous now that we are going to meet in a place where anything can happen.

We left the car on the street outside his apartment and walked to my home. It felt strange to walk beside him in a different place than at work and outdoors. The only time I have gone with him outside was when he followed me into the backyard of Vaksalagatan 25. That time I didn't think about how his presence felt, but now I did. We didn't talk, and I wondered what he was thinking and if he was as excited as I was. I couldn't decide when nothing was said, and I didn't see his face so clearly. In the car we often sit quiet, so it felt about as usual, but I didn't know.

We weren't alone in the elevator up. I came to think of how bothered Bernt used to be if there were other people who went by the same elevator as us when we visited mamma. He couldn't just stand there and wait but almost always started talking to me in a strained way, as if to show how unaffected by the situation he was. I thought he was ridiculous and never answered when he did like that. But Göran stood there without talking and seemed just as usual.

I had cleaned and tidied up before he would come. He seemed curious and walked around inspecting my things while I sat on the sofa and watched him.

– This is a lush pot-plant.

– Yes, it's a kind of lily.

– Then it fits well here with you.

– Why?

– Your name means lily. Didn't you know that? Susanne means lily.

– Does it? How do you know?

– Well, I suppose I have looked it up some time...

– What does your name mean, then?

– Farmer, peasant, agriculturist... Not quite as romantic perhaps.

It didn't feel at all like when he came to my home when I was sick and lived with Bernt on Gröna gatan. That time I wasn't prepared for him to come and had no control.

But now I had. If he had known how observed he was, and how judged he became for everything he said and did, he might have become angry. He didn't know that I the whole time was prepared for him to make a mistake and disappoint me. I was tense and a little nervous and felt dishonest. But I had to do it to dare to trust him. After all, I could have imagined all the positive things I have thought about him and totally misjudged him.

He looked extra closely at my books.

– You're interested in psychology, I notice.

– Yes, but it was long ago I read those books. I have got some of them from grandpa, so they are rather old. But I've been thinking about starting to study psychology.

– At the university?

– Yes. But I haven't applied yet, and it isn't certain I'll be accepted either. Do you have any special interests?

– No, I'm interested in most things. And I'm a qualified economist, so I have to stick to that, I suppose.

– Would you like to do something else? Don't you like your job with Egon?

– Well, it's fine. But you can never know what the future holds. If you start studying, you have to quit your job.

– Yes, or if I can take a leave.

When he saw my psychology books and I said I might be going to study, he thought I perhaps have to quit my job, and that made me happy. But it doesn't have to mean anything.

He took out some of the books in the bookcase and read on the back covers. I didn't quite remember what books I have, so afterwards I checked, and I wondered what the titles revealed and what it had made him think and believe about me. I was a bit ashamed, because I know I bought some of the books to get to know about myself and not because I was interested in understanding other people's' problems. It's true that I am interested in psychology, but the reason I bought and read psychology books, was that I wanted to find answers about myself. Göran may have understood that, and then he could also figure out what I have had, or still have, problems with. For instance, which conclusions did he draw from the fact that I have "The Hite Report" and books about abuse of women, rape, infidelity, divorce, and love?

We drank wine both with the food and afterwards, and I was affected almost immediately. I wanted to be on the alert when I asked him about the car accident, but I felt that I became a bit woozy.

And it wasn't just the wine I was affected by. When we sat on the sofa, I was so aware of his physical presence that I had to make an effort to keep my thoughts in order. We sat in each corner of the sofa, and he looked around and fortunately seemed to think of completely different things than I did.

– This is a nice apartment.

– Yes, but it's not my own. I'm just borrowing it. It's grandpa who owns it, but he is on long-term care now.

– Your boyfriend, then? Does he still live on Gröna gatan? Your ex-boyfriend, I mean.

– Yes, I guess so.

– You don't meet?

– No.

– How long were you together?

– For six years.

– Why did it end?

– He got tired of me. But it…

– You can tell me if you think I'm too inquisitive.

– No, it's okay. How about you? Have you lived with anyone?

– Yes, but it also ended.

– Why?

– I was in a car accident and became impossible to live with.

– When was it?

– It will be five years this autumn.

– Had you started working in the office then?

– When the accident occurred, you mean?

– Yes.

– Yes, I had. But I went on sick leave for quite some time afterwards.

When I was new at the office, Viola told me that Göran had been in a car accident and that his sister had died in it, so I already knew, but I didn't tell him. I didn't know any particulars, and I wanted him to tell everything himself. But as soon as he had mentioned the accident, I started asking questions about it.

– Were you seriously injured?

– No, it was mentally I was broken. My sister was with me in the car, and she didn't survive. She was so seriously injured that she died. And it was me who drove.

– How old was she?

– Seventeen.

– What was her name?

– Jenny.

– You can tell me if you don't think it concerns me, or if you don't want to talk about her.

– No, it's okay. I'm just a little unused to it. Most people tend to avoid the subject and find it unpleasant.

– Do you think so too?

– No, I think it's good to talk about difficult things you've been through.

– Mm.

– I think everyone actually needs it. And when it comes to death, I think it's good to think about it sometimes. We will all die. Death is inevitable, and it's better to accept it, and try to live with that knowledge, than to avoid the thought of it.

I didn't want to ask too much about his sister, and when he got upset and became silent, I changed the subject. I wanted him to tell from the beginning when he was ready and not feel pressured. I asked a little about his family instead.

– Do you have any more sisters or brothers?

– Yes, two older brothers.

— Do they also live here in Uppsala?

— No, one lives in Stockholm and one in Gävle. Both are married and have children.

— Your parents, then?

— They also live in Gävle. This is where I was born and raised. How about you? Do you have any brothers or sisters?

— No, I'm an only child, and my parents divorced when I was eight. But now it was you we were going to talk about.

— Well, was it? Were we?

He kindly answered all my questions, but he tried several times to transfer the attention to me. When I didn't agree to it, and directed it back to him, he smiled and looked amused. Or if he was amused that I became so talkative and different from the wine. I noticed myself that I was chattering. Then I came to think of what it was like when I drank wine with Bernt, when I needed it to be able to fall asleep in the evenings after the rape, and then I felt that sadness again, and the crying that was on its way. But I controlled myself and concentrated on what I had decided to do.

— How did the accident happen?

— Well, I… I was at home in Gävle over the weekend, and the night before Saturday I picked up Jenny at a party she had been to. It was in September, and it was about half past one at night. It was dark and rainy, but

the visibility and road conditions were good, and I didn't drive too fast. Jenny was sitting next to me in the front seat, and both of us were wearing seat belts. Sometimes when you sit beside me in the car, I come to think of… Jenny was exhilarated and happy and went on talking like she used to. Yes, and so… I saw the oncoming car in the distance and realized that it was coming towards us at very high speed. It had the headlights on, and the driver didn't dim them before the meeting – or what would have been a meeting if everything had gone as it should. Suddenly I saw it coming towards us on the wrong side of the road, and I was dazzled by the headlights and couldn't steer away. I had time to recognize that it came obliquely towards us in the direction of the ditch edge, and I threw the steering wheel to the left to avoid a collision, but it wasn't enough. It just… I heard Jenny scream before the bang and the impact came and half the front of the car was compressed. It was pushed back, but it didn't overturn and remained on the road. The other car overturned behind us in the ditch. It turned around but righted itself again and ran into a tree that stopped it. I became aware of it later. All I could think of in that moment was if Jenny had made it. She was still in her belt, but she was trapped by the compressed door and was completely… Blood was pouring out of her mouth, and I… I opened her belt and tried to pull her to me, but she was stuck and couldn't be released. I tried to straighten her head and turn it to the side so that she wouldn't be suffocated by the blood, but it just fell back. I took her hand and searched for the pulse on her wrist, but I felt no pulse beats and under-stood that she hadn't survived. Yes, and then… Then I became aware that cars had stopped, and that people were moving outside on the road. I remember the head-lights and a man opening the door on my side to help me out. I remember a voice saying that ambulances were on their way and that I should take it easy, and I remem-ber the expression on a face that turned towards Jenny and quickly withdrew again. I refused to let go of her hand and I didn't let myself be helped out of the car. I couldn't understand that she was dead while I myself sat there seemingly unharmed. Later it turned out that I had some wounds that needed to be taken care of, but all were slight, and I didn't have to stay in the hospital for any other reason than that I was shocked.

How did I feel when he told me? I noticed that he tried to present it as calmly and concisely as he could, but I saw how difficult it was for him, and I couldn't stop my tears when I saw how close to crying he himself was several times. I wanted to hold him and comfort him, but it wouldn't have been right, and I didn't say anything. I just sat there looking at him and felt how much I wanted to give him, and would have given him at once, if only he had let me do it.

He showed me a newspaper clipping about the accident, and before I read it, I came to think of my own clipping, that I let him read when he thought Bernt had beaten me. I had two clippings, but he only got to read one, and now both are gone. I thought he should get rid of his as well, as proof that he no longer blames himself. But he may do so, even though he knows it wasn't his fault that his sister died.

YOUNG WOMAN DEAD IN CAR ACCIDENT
At 00.38 a.m. on Saturday morning, SOS was alerted to a traffic accident on highway 80 west of Gävle. A car ended up on the wrong side of the road and collided head-on with another vehicle.

The consequences of the crash were fatal. Police and rescue services worked for a long time at the scene since a female passenger was trapped. They had to cut open the roof of one of the cars to free her.

– It was a heavy collision, it can be seen in the large bodywork damage to the cars, says Fredrik Nilsson at Gävle police.

A 24-year-old man and a 17-year-old woman were traveling in one car. The man, who was slightly injured, was taken by ambulance to Gävle hospital. The woman died in close connection to the collision. The driver of the oncoming car departed from the scene.

The cause of the accident must be investigated. The police conducted a site investigation immediately after what happened, and another investigation was conducted on Saturday morning in full daylight.

The circumstances mean that the Gävle police have initiated a preliminary investigation on serious case of reckless driving and manslaughter.

*– Shortly before the accident, the police received a tip
that a car was being driven at a very high speed near the
accident site, says Sonja Wiklund, head of preliminary
investigation at the Gävle police. It was a man who
called before the accident and told that he had been over-
taken by a car on highway 80. But if he is the driver who
is involved in this accident, it is too early to comment
on, says Sonja Wiklund.*

I can't imagine how awful it must have been. I
want to but I can't. It gets completely empty in me
when I try. I can see it in front of me, how he sits
there in the compressed car and holds his sister's
hand while the blood flows out of her mouth and
she dies, but I can't imagine his feelings. Shouldn't
I be able to do that? Shouldn't I at least have an
idea about it? But I haven't, and it makes me feel
bad. The only thing I have to give him is myself,
but that's not the same as understanding.

*– The person who caused the accident escaped. The guy
who owned the car had reported it stolen the same night.
He was at a party with a friend and had left the car unlocked outside for a short while, and when he came back
it was gone. The report was made about half an hour
after the accident. Sometime later, rumours began to
circulate that it was the guy himself who had driven the
car and that he had been dead drunk. But when the*

police met him after the accident, he had no visible injuries, and everyone at the party testified that he had been there all night. The car that had overturned and collided with a tree was so demolished that no one could believe he had been sitting in it at the crash, and it wasn't very likely that he would also have managed to get back to the party on foot afterwards. Still, rumours began to circulate that this was the case. I wasn't familiar with him, but I knew who he was, and he was quite notorious in the neighbourhood. He had been run in for speeding offences and drunken driving several times and some other things that I don't remember now. But the police believed him, and the insurance company believed him, and he got money paid out. That's what people had heard him sit and brag about – that he had tricked both the police and the insurance company and that he had had a guardian angel every time he had crashed his cars. My father was convinced that he was the one who had driven at the accident, and I actually thought so too, but there was nothing we could do to prove it, so it was just a matter of letting go and trying to move on.

Did I make it? Did I manage to listen to him so that it felt right and good for him? I didn't want him to regret telling me. Afterwards I asked questions, and he answered without seeming bothered or reluctant, so I assumed it had gone well. I was the first outside his family he told, he said. He hadn't even told his girlfriend. At first, he couldn't talk about it at all, and their relationship ended before he began to feel better.

– I probably didn't handle it very well. At first, I shut myself in and became speechless. I built a wall around me that no one could get through. I had difficulty meeting others who just went on with their lives as if nothing had happened. I couldn't bear to talk about Jenny's death. Then it was as if a trapdoor opened under me and I fell into an abyss. I realized that she was gone and that the only thing I could do was accept it and take the pain. I tried to stick to what I knew was true, that mental pain heals you if you just stay in it and experience it. I forced myself to endure, no matter how bad it hurt, and after a while I began to feel better. When you and I met, when you started working for Egon, it had been just over a year, so the worst was probably over by then, but it's said that it takes several years to get through the first grief when you've lost a close relative. The process continues after that as well, although it may not be noticeable so much externally anymore. And it was probably a little extra difficult for me considering the so-called survivor guilt that said that I should have died too, or that I should have died instead of her.

When we had finished talking about the accident, it was as if we couldn't take it anymore. We finished the wine that was left, and Göran apologized for the gloomy atmosphere. But it wasn't his fault, and I said so, because it was I who had asked him to tell. I hadn't expected anything else since I had planned it that way. I had a bad conscience because I had made him depressed, but there was no other way to do it. And he said he thinks it's good to talk about difficult things that you have been through. But then maybe it was me he was thinking of and not himself.

I had no thoughts about sex while we talked, nor afterwards. I don't think he had either. We were both tired and just wanted to be alone. Anyway, that's how it felt when he got up and left.

Later, when I was in bed, I started crying and thought: *I can't handle this, I can't handle this!* It felt like I was close to drowning in sadness and despair.

What is it that I can't handle? Don't I have the strength to be aware of and think about what he has been through? Is it too much for me? Am I too weak? Can't I care about him?

But I want to. I must. I will.

I thought Göran would invite me back, but he hasn't. Doesn't he want it to continue? For every day that goes by without him asking, I get more and more disappointed and think I may have been mistaken about him after all. Sometimes I think I can let go, but then I get angry and sad again and feel trapped because I can't stop waiting.

I have decided not to protect myself from the truth, so instead of getting angry and feeling cheated, I cry. Every evening when I get home I cry. In the daytime, when I meet him at work, I make an effort not to show how I feel and not to avoid him, as I did before as soon as I became unsure. That I invited him to me, and asked him to tell me about the accident, wasn't because I hoped he would show interest in me in return. I did it because I want to get to know him, and if he doesn't feel the same for me, I have to accept it. I know that. But I can't know for sure that that's the way it is, and I can't stand not knowing.

Why doesn't he invite me back? Does he regret coming to my home? Does he regret telling me about the car accident? Was he disappointed in how I behaved? Did he think I was drinking too much? Doesn't he want it to be more than what we have at work? Isn't he interested in me, or is he afraid I will say no? Is he as unsure of me as I am of him? Doesn't he understand what I want?

When it was over between Bernt and me, I stopped taking birth control pills. Now I have started again. No matter how uncertain I am about how it will be, I want to be ready and prepared for everything.

PART THREE

I tried as long as possible to wait, but at last I couldn't stand it any longer. One day when Göran drove me home and we were in the car, I said:

"On Friday, it's your turn to offer pizza. If it suites you and you want to?"

I said it quickly and tried to make it sound cheerful and natural. It wasn't easy for me to ask, but I could no longer just wait and not know. I had thought out exactly what to say, and I looked at him the whole time as I said it to see in his face how he reacted. I was afraid he would feel pressured and accept it only out of politeness.

But he didn't. He smiled. He became happy and smiled.

"Yes, I want to, and it suits me well," he said. "I was going to suggest it myself, but I thought you might be a little tired of me after my long accounts last time."

"No, I was the one who asked," I said. "I wanted to know."

"Yes, I got to compensate you in some way," he said and smiled again.

What did he mean by that? What my body thought he meant, and reacted to in a flash, didn't have to be true.

To be sensible, however, I have decided that the compensation should be mental. I will tell him about the rape and see if he can listen without reacting strangely.

What if he can't make it? What if he asks the wrong kind of questions? What if I will feel superior to him, as I felt superior to Bernt? What if he no longer wants to know?

I have rejected him twice when he has asked me about it, and I can't hope he will bring it up a third time. I must do it myself. I want to prove to both him and myself that I can tell it without being ashamed of how I reacted and that I am free from it now.

I should be able to tell anyone. Mamma, grandpa, Egon, Viola… I should be able to stand on a stage and tell the whole world. So strong, and so sure of where the guilt lies, I should be.

But I don't know if I am. If I tell, I shouldn't keep some of it to myself, as if I share a secret with... the *perpetrator* and protect him, should I? Admittedly, he said at the trial that he didn't remember me, but it shouldn't just be me who knows and remembers what he did, should it? Shouldn't everyone get to know it?

I don't know what to call him. From the beginning I said "that guy", "the guy in town", or "he who did it", but it feels way too nice now, and his name, once I got to know it, I have never been able to use. So, what should I call him when I talk about him? The perpetrator? The rapist? The creep? The swine? The shit? The zilch?

No word feels right, because just to mention him is like a confirmation that he exists, and I don't want him to do that.

The thoughts of him make it start creeping inside me with irritation. I feel my muscles tense, as if I am ready to attack, and I am filled with anger and think: *Go to hell, you bastard! You must go!* In a brief glance, I remember kicking Bernt away from me, but it's not him it's about now.

I haven't hated him yet. I think I can avoid hatred by pretending that he doesn't exist. That's why I don't know what to call him. I am not done with him at all. I am just deceiving myself.

But now I at least know that I am mad at him and think he is a bastard who should stay away from me. That may be enough. I may not have to hate him if I just feel aggressive and defensive when I think of him.

That's how I should have felt from the beginning. That's how I should have felt. If I had done that, it would never have happened.

But I was neither angry nor afraid. Would it have been better if I had been afraid?

Fear can build up in the muscles. If the muscles can't be controlled by the will, it doesn't help to want to do something. I have read it in a book. You must not let fear take over. Instead, you should let the energy that lies in fear turn into rage. And then you should roar. At the same time as you roar, you should coordinate your movements so that you are able to both kick and use your hands to scratch the attacker in the face or run your thumbs into his eyes. And then, once you have got him off balance, you can escape.

If I had had sense enough to be afraid, I might have done so. But I did almost nothing at all to get away because I wasn't able to feel what I should have felt.

When we were in the car on our way home to Göran, I wondered to myself if we would get wine with the food this time as well, like at my home, or if he had decided that we would be without. Actually, I don't know how fond of wine he is. At my home, he only drank a few glasses, and he may have done so mostly out of politeness. But I thought it might be easier for me to talk about the rape if I had drunk a little and hoped there would be wine.

He parked the car on the street below his apartment. It's located at the top of a three-storey building. You enter from the courtyard, where the nine-storey houses on Ritargatan are located. He went before me up the stairs and unlocked the door to the apartment and held it open for me.

His apartment is a two-room flat with a kitchenette, and it has a balcony facing the street and Vaksala church. In the living room, he has a dining table and two chairs, a long bookshelf, a sofa set, a swivel armchair, a floor lamp, and a TV. There are paintings and potted plants but no photographs

and almost no ornaments. I didn't think of curtains
and carpets. In the bedroom he has a wide bed
with a dark green bedspread and purple decora-
tive pillows, a wall shelf, and a chest of drawers.

It turned out as I had hoped that we got wine
with the food. After eating, we sat down at the coffee table and continued drinking. We sat on the
sofa and talked, and finally the conversation got
on to the rape.

– How long have you lived here?

– For four years.

– Have you lived alone all along?

– Yes, in this apartment I have always lived alone.

*– Where did you live before? Or the two of you, I
mean.*

– In Eriksberg.

– Are you still meeting her?

– No, I'm not. She has a new boyfriend now.

*– Did you take it hard? That she couldn't cope with
you, I mean.*

– Yes, I probably did. But I understood her too.

– How long had you been together?

*– For three years. But you never told me why it ended
between you and… Bernt?*

*– No. It was because of how he reacted to the rape.
That's when I realized that it wasn't all right between
us.*

The rape. I managed to overcome my resistance to

saying the word out loud and made it sound natural and easy.

Now he would come to know that it was a completed rape. Now I would come to know if he could listen.

When I said the word, I watched him closely, and I saw that he got a wondering expression on his face.

"The rape?" he said. "I thought you got away?" He said it so naturally, as if it were any ordinary word, and I felt that he didn't defend himself.

– Do you remember what was in the newspaper notice I showed you when you came to my home when I was sick?

– Yes.

– It said I got away, but I didn't. I thought so at first, but I didn't. And do you remember when you followed me into the yard where it happened?

– Yes, I do.

– That I was so upset that time, was because I remembered how it had really happened. You held your arms round me and tried to comfort me, but I couldn't receive it even though I wanted to, and when you asked if I wanted to talk about it, I couldn't do that either. But it wasn't your fault.

– No, I didn't think so either.

– What did you think, then?

– That you couldn't.

– Didn't you take it personally that I rejected you?

– I didn't feel rejected. You had shown confidence in me by asking me to come with you into the yard, and I thought you would have told me if you had been able to. That you actually wanted to.

– Yes, I did. But there was so much more…

– Mm.

– Did you know that?

– Yes, I felt that you had things to sort out.

– How could you feel that?

– I noticed it from your behaviour.

– What did you think when you noticed how crazy I was?

– I didn't think you were crazy. I know myself how difficult it is to be able to take in everything at once.

– But what you thought I had been through was just a trifle compared to yours.

– But as it turned out, it was no trifle, was it?

– No.

He made it. He managed to listen to me and keep himself out. When he mentioned himself, it was just to show that he knew how it can be.

I started crying when I felt that he understood me, and that he has understood me all along, and I thought I had already received proof that he can handle it. But he didn't know what was to come. He could reach a point where it became too much for him. I could also reach a point where I could no longer stay on the right side. It was as much about me as it was about him.

And he continued.

– How did it start?
– It started with me walking past him on the street and that he came after me and asked what time it was. Then he got me into that yard.
– Mm.
– You have to ask, because I don't know how detailed you want me to tell.
– You don't have to do this if you don't want to.
– No, I know.
– But…?
– I don't know how important it is that I tell it.
– To you or to me?
– To both.
– No, neither do I.

But suddenly it didn't feel important any longer. What does it matter what happened? I thought. Why does he need to know? Isn't it enough that I know myself and forget it?

Or was I afraid? Göran noticed that I hesitated and sat quiet and waited. I had difficulty in continuing. But he helped me move on.

– I may be wrong, but I think it would be good if you told me anyway.
– Do you?
– Yes. But only if you feel that you really can and want to.

– I don't really know what I'm feeling right now. But I don't mind you asking.

– Okay. Then I start with… What kind of person was he, that guy? You said before, after the trial, that he had raped others? So, he was some kind of serial rapist who engaged in assault rapes?

– Yes, he must have been. I have never thought about that.

– How old was he?

– I don't remember. Between twenty and twenty-five, I think.

– What was he sentenced to?

– I don't know. I never found out.

– Why not?

– I didn't want to be interested in him.

– No, I understand that. But you know you can request the verdict if you would like to read it?

– Yes, I might do it sometime. But not now.

– What do you remember most clearly from what happened?

– That he smeared my face with his penis.

– How did he do it?

– Pressed and rubbed it against my cheeks and tried to force it into my mouth.

– Why do you remember just that, do you think?

– Because it was so disgusting and because my face smelled so bad afterwards. From the beginning I didn't know what it was due to, but when I sat at the police station, I smelled it.

He asked the right kind of questions the whole time and was interested in my answers. First, he asked a little about the guy, but it wasn't him he was interested in, but me. That's how it felt anyway, and that's what made my resistance go away. The wine I was drinking also helped.

– Did he threaten you?
– Yes.
– How?
– He said he had a gun, and he said he would hit me, and he said that if I screamed or didn't open my mouth, he would kill me.
– Did he have a weapon? A gun?
– Yes, he said that, but I never saw it.
– Did he use… What kind of violence did he use?
– He pushed me and held me and banged my head against a wall and gave me a box on the ear and pried my legs apart and threw me on the ground and gave me a punch in the face.
– Yes, I saw that you were injured, but I didn't understand how much. Your whole body must have been… You must have been bruised all over.
– Yes, I was.

When we talked about how injured I had become, I began to cry, because then I realized how unfair and terrible it was that I was beaten. I felt that Göran wanted to comfort me, but he didn't. He was silent and just waited until he saw that I was ready to go on.

"And then he came into you?" he said, and my body didn't understand that it was the rape we were talking about but reacted as if it was *he* who would come into me. His words caused a wave of arousal to well up in me, and I didn't understand how it could happen when we talked about such negative things. But I didn't show anything and tried to pull myself together. Then I came to think of how the policeman who interrogated me expressed himself about the same thing. He almost made it sound like it wasn't about me.

"And then he inserted his penis into the vagina?" he said.

I remember reacting to it and thinking that maybe he chose to say it in an indefinite way so as not to get too personal. "Whose vagina?" I wanted to ask. And "insert" was a far too gentle word. Why did Göran also express it far too gently? Why did he say "come in" as if I welcomed it?

It was because it sounded positive that my body reacted the way it did. But why did he say so? Not because he thought I wanted it anyway, as Bernt seemed to believe. I knew he didn't mean that.

But as soon as my thoughts had caught up with my body, I reacted.

"Come in, as welcome in, you mean?" I said.

It slipped out of me before I had time to stop myself, and I heard for myself how cold my voice sounded. How could I be so hard and unfair to him? Why did I expect him to be perfect and not be able to make the slightest mistake? That he chose the wrong words just because he was influenced by his own feelings, which I am almost sure he was, wasn't something I had to get hung up on, was it? Because it was the same for me, that even though we talked about other things, I was constantly affected by his physical presence.

How could I explain to him that my negative reaction was due to the fact that I was testing him, and that I was oversensitive to the slightest mistake?

"I'm sorry," I said. "I know you didn't mean it that way."

"No, I'm the one to ask for forgiveness. I was a little distracted… I know he raped you."

I could have asked what had distracted him, but I didn't. I only thought he might be as confused as I was and regretted that I had questioned him.

I became more and more affected by the wine, and when I tried to see in his face how he reacted to what I said, I had difficulty focusing. He sat looking down at his glass and didn't watch me. I felt him listening, and when I became silent, he looked up. His expression was open and serious and not at all like Bernt's cold, stiff mask that he always hid behind when he felt threatened or uneasy. Göran remained open and he didn't distance himself from me or suspect me of participation as Bernt did.

Bernt and I lived together when it happened, and perhaps that's a difference, but it shouldn't have been. If we had been together out of love, he would have reacted differently. But it wasn't out of love we were together. I know that now. At that time, I didn't understand better and agreed to things that I actually didn't want to participate in. It wasn't his fault, and I am not angry with him anymore, but I never want to see him again.

"You like to be raped," was the last thing he said to me before he disappeared.

– What happened inside the yard?

– First, we stood by a wall. He pushed me up against a wall and took off my coat, trousers, and briefs. It was my own fault that he could do it. But then I got loose and ran away. I thought I had got away then and forgot the rest. That's what came back to me when you and I were there. When I ran away, he grabbed me again and threw me to the ground and sat on me. He rubbed himself against my face and tried to force me to suck. When I refused, he punched me in the face. Now I'm just telling you so that you don't have to ask and don't have to weigh every word before you answer just because I'm testing you.

– Testing me? Well… okay.

– He had no erection, but he got one when he had been rubbing for a while, and then he forced himself in and started bumping, and I didn't scream, because then he would have hit me, and he had difficulty ejaculating and

exerted himself so he became sweaty, and then I was gone for a while, and then he jumped up and disappeared. That's how it happened, and you and the police are the only ones who have been told, for no one else has wanted to know, and now I'm not going to drink any more, because now it feels a little foggy, and I don't really know what I'm saying.

– *How about Bernt, then? Didn't you tell him?*

– *No, I didn't, because he was the same.*

– *He was?*

– *Yes, but he couldn't help it.*

– *What happened when he had disappeared, then?*

– *Bernt?*

– *No, the guy who raped you.*

– *Then I tried to get up, and then I fainted, and then a guy came and helped me into Lucullus and called the police. Then I still thought I had got away.*

– *Mm.*

– *Then I lied to the police.*

– *But if you didn't remember, one can't say that you lied.*

– *No, about other things.*

– *You lied about other things?*

– *Now you sound like a cop. You ask like a cop.*

– *I do?*

– *Yes, you would be a good interrogator. You're the one who has made me tell.*

– *Was it your intention that I should get to know, or did it just happen, because of the wine or my excellent interrogation technique?*

– It was my intention.

– Was that the test?

– Yes.

– Did I make it, then?

– Yes, you did, because you're perfect. Do you still have the tape with Arne Lamberth that we listened to in the car before?

– Yes, it's still in the glove compartment.

– Then we'll listen to it next time we go, because it's a long time since we listened to it, and you're like a song on that tape.

– Am I like a song on the tape with Arne Lamberth?

– Yes, you are. You're like Russ… Russian Folk Song. But now I'm not going to drink any more, because I talk so much nonsense, and you never know what I can come out with, because I trust you and could tell you anything. I can happen to say too much, and I don't want to do that, so now I had better go home before I happen to say too much.

I shouldn't have drunk so much, because towards the end I had to pay attention to myself the whole time not to say what I was thinking and feeling. *I trust you, I'm in love with you, I want to sleep with you, I love you,* I thought.

When I was about to leave, he followed me across the street to my gate. There he hugged me, as you hug any friend, and then I was glad I had managed to keep my words back.

Now he knows. I had to tell, and we both made it, but now I never want to talk about it again. I am dead tired of it, after all the time I have spent on it and after all the space it has been allowed to take in my life. It doesn't matter anymore. I just want to forget it.

Now he knows, but it still doesn't feel good and I don't understand why. Why am I not satisfied?

I didn't tell it with feeling. I just rattled it off as if to get it over with. That wasn't how I had meant it to be.

The way I said it made me unable to receive comfort. I thought I didn't need comfort, but I do. No one has comforted me for what happened. Göran has tried, but I haven't been open and able to receive it, and I wasn't this time either.

It makes me sad. Why do I hinder myself from getting what I need? That's not right. I must let him comfort me! That's what he wants and that's what I need.

A few days after the rape, I went into his room at work when he wasn't there and just stood in the middle of the floor thinking about him. If he had come then, I might have let him comfort and help me. But I knew he was free from work and wouldn't come.

Now I know I can trust him. I know him. I know who he is.

Why do I cry when I think that? Because I didn't see him before, even though he was there? Because I was so far away from myself that I wasn't *able* to see him?

It feels as if he has been waiting for me all this long time. Waiting for me to discover him and feel that he understood and was willing to listen to me as soon as I was ready to tell.

It's my fault that he has had to wait. Perhaps that's why I am sad. I didn't want to do that to him. Nor did I want to do it to myself. I didn't want to do it to *us*.

No, I can't know for sure that he has been waiting. I can't know for sure that he wants the same as I do. All I know is that he said he felt I had things to sort out. That he noticed it from my behaviour. But that doesn't have to mean that he was waiting.

I went to Göran in his room at work and closed the door after me. He was sitting in his chair behind the desk, and I sat in the visitor's chair opposite him.

"Sorry for last Friday," I said. "It didn't go well."

I wanted to explain, and I wanted to show him that I am open now. At the same time, I was afraid of what could happen if he touched me. Would the consolation turn into sex then? I didn't want that, and I didn't trust myself. I didn't trust my body. I knew I could control myself and hide it, but how could I receive comfort if I was sexually aroused? Wouldn't that hinder as much as if I were closed?

Göran paused his work and looked at me.

– What didn't go well?

– How I told it. I wasn't open.

– No? Do you regret telling me?

– No, but I shouldn't have reeled it out like I did, as if it were of no importance. I shouldn't have drunk so much wine.

– No?

– I wasn't honest with how I feel.

– How do you feel, then?

– That I'm sorry I was beaten and raped. I have diffi-culty feeling it. That's why I'm closed and impassive when I talk about it. Yes, that's what I wanted to say. So that you don't think I…

I took courage and tried. When I had said what I had intended to say and got up from the chair, he also rose and came up to me and hugged me. When I felt his arms around me, I began to cry. He held my head against his shoulder and his arm around my back while I cried.

He was close to me. He held me close to him. I felt his warm body against mine, and I pressed myself against him and cried and let him comfort me. I received his comfort, and it hurt so much as if I had never been physically comforted before. I might not have been either. I may not have been.

In the car, Göran put on the tape with Arne Lamberth, and when Russian Folk Song came, he looked at me and smiled. I knew he was thinking of what I had said about him being like that song, and it made me feel a little stupid. But he didn't mean to embarrass me.

Previously, when I listened to it, I was always ready to cry, but now I didn't feel that way. I am not feeling that way any longer. I still find it sad and beautiful, but I don't start crying when I hear it.

When the music had stopped, he started asking me questions.

– I've been thinking about what you told me last Friday. You disappeared so quickly that I didn't have time to ask about things I was wondering about.

– Then you can do it now.

– Yes, you said nothing about the hospital, for instance, about what it was like when you came to the hospital.

– I never got there. I didn't need it.

– You didn't need it?

– No, a doctor came to the police station and examined me there instead.

– Well… Is that how it's usually done?

– I don't know. But at that time no one knew it was a completed rape. Maybe it was because of that.

– Mm. Were you treated well by the police, then?

– Yes, they took it more seriously than I did myself. I was so stupid…

– How do you mean?

– I diminished it and almost didn't even consider it a crime. Well, later, when I remembered everything, I did, but not from the beginning.

– Why did you do that?

– It's hard to explain.

– Try.

– It had to do with my and Bernt's relationship. Or how he looked at… No, I'm not to blame him. Most of it probably had to do with my childhood.

– How?

– Well, that I didn't feel worth very much.

– How did Bernt react to the fact that you had been raped, then?

– I never told him. He read what was in the newspaper, what you also got to read, that it was just an attempted rape, and that's all he knew.

– But when the trial took place, then? Then he must have found out?

– No, I received a letter with a summons, and I didn't show it to him, and later, when the trial took place, I had *already moved away from him.*

– Who helped you afterwards? Who could you talk to later?

– No one. I wanted to tell you, but at that time, when it had recently happened, I couldn't, and then it felt like it wasn't needed. I sorted it out myself.

– Mm.

– Like you did with yours.

– Mm.

I hadn't intended to tell him about my weird thoughts and feelings, but when he asked, I got into it anyway. It felt good that he wanted to know more, and that we could talk about private things in the car as well, because we have almost never done that before. The car has only been like an empty, common space, and that space we filled with ourselves now. We expanded our contact opportunities, and that's how I wanted it to be when I decided to approach him. And it feels easier to keep to the point when we sit in the car where not much else can happen.

– Do you think a lot about what happened?

– No, not any longer. But in the beginning, I dwelled on it all the time. The worst thing was almost that I didn't understand my own feelings. That I thought I reacted abnormally. That I couldn't feel hurt and humiliated even though I knew I had become so. I had to find out what was wrong with me, and that overshadowed

almost everything else in the beginning.

— You weren't just shocked, then?

— No, it wasn't just that. I was shocked too, as if I had been in an accident, but it wasn't just that. I have had to struggle to put all the blame on the right person, and to feel how I really reacted to what he did to me. That's what has been difficult.

— And how do you feel now when you think of him?

— Anger, resistance and… defence readiness.

— Good.

When we talked about the rape, I got sad several times. The difference between what I feel now, which is right, and what I felt then, which was wrong, is so great. Now that I know how it feels when I really want to, I also know how it feels when I don't want to at all. At that time, I didn't.

— Were you afraid?

— No, I wasn't, and that's also part of the abnormal.

— How do you mean?

— I should have been frightened, but I wasn't, and that's not normal.

— But he threatened you with a weapon?

— He had no weapon, and I knew that. Or I didn't know, but I didn't believe him when he claimed it, because he didn't show it. He just pushed his jacket out with a finger from inside a pocket.

— But then…

— Oh, you don't know how stupid I was! In every

way possible. I can hardly bear to think about it!

His questions made me start to cry, and that was good, I suppose, because it showed that I was open. But I was ashamed when I thought about how stupid I was and how strange I reacted both before and after the rape.

Göran helps me feel by asking questions that no one else has asked, and that's good for me. I know that. But I don't want it to be just about me when we talk. I can be self-absorbed when I am alone.

But it's he who asks, and he doesn't do so out of politeness. He is interested in me and wants to know. I must trust it and not feel guilty because I need and receive what he gives me. What's wrong with me? I even felt guilty when I was with the police because I took up their time and was a bother to them.

PART FOUR

I am thinking of Göran. Now that I know what it looks like in his home, I can see him standing in the kitchenette or sitting at the table in the living room or in the swivel chair in front of the TV or lying on the bed in the bedroom. I see him walking around in the apartment, and he is as lonely as I am.

Is he thinking of me? Does he wonder what I am doing? Does he long for me as I long for him, and always have, even though I haven't understood? Is he thinking of his sister? Is he crying?

No, I'm the only one who cries; any time, anyhow, every day.

We live so close, and yet we are in different places all the time when we are not at work. It doesn't feel right.

At work we behave just as usual, as if nothing has happened. Egon and Viola don't notice that it is a different situation now. Or isn't it? Have we just… *unburdened* ourselves, and so it is no more? I might just imagine there is more. I may be so filled with my feelings for him that I don't perceive *his* feelings. He passed my silly test, and he has listened kindly and understandingly to me, and he has comforted me, but I don't know more than that. Maybe the rest is just mine. My excitement and my fantasies about us are perhaps just a reaction to the fact that I have been so closed before. What I feel may not be mutual at all.

I have browsed some of the books I have got from grandpa, and in the book "The Betrayal of the Body" by Alexander Lowen it says:

A human being is responsible for his actions but not for his emotions. An emotion is a biological reaction in the body, which is outside the power of the self. The role of the self is to experience the feeling, not to judge or control it. What is within the control of the self is the action. A healthy person who is angry or sexually aroused is able to control his emotions until he gets a suitable opportunity to express them. That way, he can act responsibly. A healthy self is not helpless in relation to the body. If it would cause harm to express the feeling in words or deeds, the self can hold back this expression through its control over the will muscles without at the same time having to deny or suppress the feeling. In this way, the damage is avoided without any inner conflict.

I started crying when I read it, because that's how everyone should behave, but many don't do it.

I want to give Göran everything I have. I want

to give myself to him. I want to receive him. I want him to come into me. That it doesn't happen is almost unbearable. It *must* happen. There is no other possibility.

It's when I am alone and think of him that I release it. Not at work and almost never in the car, although we are always alone there. I only do it at home. Sometimes I can hardly stand it. It almost doesn't help that I masturbate, because my body is set on him all the time, and just thinking of him, makes it ready again.

I didn't know it could feel like this. With Bernt, I had no desire at all and thought I was frigid. But that's not the case. I am not. I know that for sure now.

Last night I dreamed of papa. I don't remember what it was, except that he locked me in a big box and that I submitted to it without protesting.

I was only eight years old when he disappeared. I barely remember him. It was he who wanted to divorce mamma, and I understand that, because she probably left no room for him either.

He was in the military. When I was little, I was afraid of him. He was so stern in his manner, and when I sought contact with him, he almost always dismissed me. For instance, if I had fallen and hurt myself, and I ran to him for comfort, he could say: "This is nothing to cry about," or "This couldn't have hurt very much." He never had time with me and didn't care about me. When he disappeared, I didn't miss him, because I had never had him.

And mamma wasn't there either. It was only when I was sick and lying in bed that she could look after me a little and care about my feelings. Otherwise, I was always alone.

It's because of what I experienced when I was little that I became so weird later. It's almost the worst, and what I am most ashamed of. Do I have to tell Göran about all the weird thoughts and fantasies I had and maybe still have? I have already mentioned some, but I haven't revealed everything. I may not have to do it either.

And how were *his* parents? What kind of childhood did *he* have? There is so much I still don't know about him. There is so much left to find out.

What I do know is that his father is an agronomist and that his mother is an archive administrator at Gävle district court. I know he has two older brothers alive, and a younger sister who is dead. I know he moved away from home when he was nineteen years old and that he studied business administration at Uppsala university. That he has a good all-round education but is non-technical. That he likes to wash, clean, and cook. That he has a boiled egg and oatmeal porridge with milk for breakfast. That he gets annoyed at impractical things that are not functionally designed. That he likes plants and animals, pizza, coffee, scones, whipped cream, nuts, classical music, and reading. That he plays tennis and swims. That he doesn't smoke, take snuff or drink hard liquor. That he detests crowds, parties, stunts, motorsports, boxing, animal cruelty and violence. Some of it he has told me himself, but most of it I have snatched up at work and memorized.

In the car on the way home, Göran suddenly said:

"Do you feel like coming to my place on Saturday evening?"

As soon as I understood what he was asking, a warm, sucking wave welled up in me. How could my body react before I even had time to think about what could happen if we met at his home?

Feel like coming.

"Yes, I do," I said.

"Good," he said and smiled. "Shall we say at seven o'clock?"

Tomorrow he is away for a conference, so we won't meet again until Saturday. In other words, I have plenty of time to get worked up and get nervous.

Because I know the time has come now. There is nothing to stop it any longer. As soon as I think about it, I get aroused.

Is it normal to react the way I do? Sometimes I think it's so exaggerated, like I am obsessed with him, or obsessed with sex. Do I feel too much now, just because I felt too little with Bernt? Am I as crazy now as I was then, but in a different way?

It might calm down once we have done it. Or how will it be? I feel so inexperienced and stupid. I have had sex with only one guy in my life, and it was never good. For six years it was that way and I thought there was something wrong with me who never felt desire. In the books I read, I found no answers. I was pathetic, and maybe I still am.

How can I be so sure he wants me? It feels as if he has decided on me and is just waiting for me to decide on him too, but that's perhaps only imagination.

My body has decided on him a long time ago. It's in my mind I am unsure. The physical takes over, so it becomes unclear to me how he is as a person. I can't really see him. The only thing I can do is receive him physically. That I want to do it may mean that I love him, but I have no clear idea about it.

Or it means that I can't resist that I am feeling loved by him. It's that feeling that makes me not doubt what he wants. For his part, there is no doubt at all, and it makes me feel safe but at the same time a little inferior and pathetic. I feel that I don't have everything needed to correspond to him.

As soon as I had hung up my things in the hall, he stood in front of me and embraced me. We were standing in the middle of the floor under the lamp, and I could hardly breathe. He was wearing black jeans and a clear blue shirt. The jeans matched his hair and the shirt his eyes. I wondered if it was deliberate, or if it had just happened to be that way. At work he sometimes wears a shirt, tie, and suit, and it makes him look different.

I also wore jeans, but blue, and a grey long-sleeved sweater. It hadn't felt right to dress up, so I hadn't done so. I am not that interested in clothes either.

As I stood there in his arms, I came to think of how stiff I had been both times before, and how different it felt now. When he kissed me, I noticed he was hard, and I pressed myself against it and kissed him back. It was the first time I answered a kiss because I wanted to. When Bernt kissed me, I almost thought it was disgusting and had to make an effort not to show it.

I could have gone straight into the bedroom

with Göran, but he wasn't in such a hurry, because he let me go and went to the kitchenette and started making coffee instead. I had to calm down and wait.

We each got a Napoleon cake with the coffee. I know that I once said at work that that sort is my favourite, and he might have remembered that.

After we had had coffee, he asked if I wanted to play Genius. The game was newly purchased, so he had no advantage from having played it before, he said. And it went well for me, even though I am not at all as all-around educated as he is.

We played for a long time, and in the end, it felt almost unbearable to sit there and just postpone what we knew would happen. Sometimes I forgot about it, because I got so absorbed in the game, but it was there the entire time.

At about half past nine we couldn't take it any longer. Then we had tea and hot sandwiches, and after that it was time. When we had cleaned the table and I was standing at the bench in the kitchenette, he came and stood behind me and embraced me. He pressed me against him and kissed my neck, and I felt he was hard.

I don't know how we got into the bedroom and got our clothes off. I was so aroused that I didn't think of it.

He caressed me and kissed me and looked at me. I felt… *cherished* by him. It was good that he didn't ask if what we were doing was difficult for me in view of the rape, because I wanted him to trust that I could keep it out. And he noticed how aroused I was. He seemed amused by it, as if the thought that he was the cause of it made him happy.

As he slid into me, I began to cry. Oh, now he is finally here, now he is finally inside me, now we are finally as close as we can get, I thought.

He moved slowly and gently, and sometimes he just lay still and looked at me. It was so delightful to have him in me, to have him there and know that there was where he wanted to be.

I did things I had never done before. I put my legs around his waist to keep him in me. I grabbed his hair with my hands. I sucked his lower lip into my mouth. I moaned and whimpered and wailed.

He doesn't know how cold and dead I was with Bernt. What if he believes I reacted like this when Bernt had sex with me too, I thought. I don't want him to believe that. He must not do that. As I am now, I am just with him. Everything is caused by him. Does he understand that? Does he know that? No one but hirn could make me feel and be like this.

When I came, I moaned, and then I cried again, and he kissed away my tears and held me.

When he had fallen asleep, I lay with my back pressed against him and felt his heart beating. I was anxious and couldn't relax and sleep. I thought that what had happened could only happen once and never again. As if it were not the beginning but the end of it all. Perhaps I have just used him to prove things to myself, and now that I have got everything I wanted, I will lose interest in him, I thought. I may not love him at all. Perhaps I imagined so just because I was physically attracted to him.

When I thought about staying with him and sleeping in his bed all night and then waking up and having breakfast with him, it felt like I couldn't do it. Getting up and getting dressed didn't feel right either. I couldn't explain to him why I had to go, and I wasn't sure that was what I wanted to do. I felt trapped and almost seized by panic.

I tried to calm down by thinking that maybe it was my thoughts that were wrong, and that I shouldn't doubt my feelings for him but hold on to what I have felt all along.

I started crying and thought I had let both him and myself down. At the same time as I was feeling remorseful, I realized I was afraid. I was afraid it was over and that I had imagined everything.

But I hadn't. I haven't. I love him. It's so strong and intense and great and deep that it hurts. Sometimes I can't bear it, but that's the truth.

Finally, I fell asleep anyway and slept all night. When I woke up and saw him beside me and remembered what we had done, I wanted it again. No foreplay was needed, because we were both just as ready, and it was just as delightful as the night before.

Afterwards, I wasn't afraid anymore and decided to take a place and feel at home with him. He gave me that place, and I took it and intend to keep it. I won't doubt what I feel anymore. If it gets weaker sometimes, or even disappears because I think wrongly, I don't need to be afraid, because now I know it will come back only if I believe in and hold on to what's true.

Either I feel sorrow and pain, or I am sexually aroused. It's only at work, where I have to think about other things, that I calm down a bit. If I am grieving that I have let myself down, it should cease now when I am not doing it anymore, shouldn't it? And why do I have to feel so aroused all the time?

His scent has stuck in my pillow and my sheets. Sometimes when I am lying on my back in bed, I part my legs, though he isn't here, and feel that I want him on top of me and inside me. I feel supple and lithe, like a cat lying and stretching itself out in the sun, waiting to be caressed. I feel pretty. I may not be, but that's how it feels.

Who else has he been with? I would ask him that, I decided. And what friends he has.

It felt like I was going to test him again. Test or interrogate. It made me feel calculating and lousy. But how else would I know? And I wanted to test myself to find out if I would get jealous or not.

– List all the girls you have been together with after high

school.

– After high school? Okay, let' see… First it was Sara, then it was Margareta, then Johanna, then Magdalena, then Emma, then Kristina…

– No, that's the ladies' week!

– Yes, you're right about that.

– You have to be serious.

– Yes, okay. Before Therese, there were actually only two. In high school I went in for tennis and didn't have time with girls. Besides, I was pimply and shy. But then I met Linda, and after her came Anna.

– How… No, this doesn't work.

– What doesn't work?

– I thought I was interested in your exes, but I'm not.

– Good.

– Why is that?

– Because neither am I.

Linda, Anna and Therese were before me. Now it's just me. He loves me. He hasn't said it, but I know it anyway. I can't feel jealous of his former girlfriends when I so clearly notice how uninterested he is in letting his thoughts go back to them.

If he met another, now that he and I are together and he wanted to leave me, I wouldn't be jealous either. He must be allowed to do what's right for him. I would never try to persuade or compel him to stay with me. I want him to feel free. Everything he does in relation to me must be of free will, because otherwise it isn't worth anything.

Grandpa has asked me if I want to buy his apartment, and I do. I get it very cheap, because soon he will die and doesn't need any money, he says. And what I pay to him, mamma will inherit, and she also has enough to get along on and doesn't need more money either, he thinks.

When the apartment is mine, Göran and I can move together. We have been able to do it all the time, in his flat, but mine is a two-room apartment with a real kitchen where you can sit and eat, so if we were to move together, I think we should live in mine. We haven't talked about it, and I don't intend to bring it up, because there is no hurry. But later on, maybe we will do it, and then it's good that I own my apartment.

Poor grandpa who is old and sick. I visit him sometimes, but now I have to do it more often, if he feels he will soon die.

Grandpa is probably the only one in my family who has cared about me. He has always talked to me and listened to me. It's from him I have got all unusual words that appear in my head from time to time. Grandma was sick and died when I was little, so I barely remember her. I asked grandpa about her last time I met him.

– *What did grandma die of?*

  – Well, my dear child… We said it was pneumonia, but so well it wasn't, I was about to say.

  – What was it then?

  – She committed suicide.

  – Oh, did she? How old was she when it happened?

  – She had just turned fifty-three.

  – Why did she do it?

  – Yes, what triggered it, we never got real clarity in. But she had been ill from time to time ever since your mother was born, and when she began to approach her menopause, it became worse. She had a depression that was so deep and severe that I didn't dare take on my responsibility to keep her at home. I turned to Ulleråker, where she had been admitted several times before and become better. In my stupidity, I thought it would be the same again, but the treatment I thought she was getting took time, and after a while I noticed that she was becoming more and more institutionalized. She didn't get better but rather worse, and finally I decided to take her home again. I wrote a series of articles about that later, about how mental hospitals were just soulless storage places for the mentally ill. Yes, and they probably still are, I guess. You give pills but no care, and that's not what it's meant to be.

  – Did it happen at home?

– Yes, she took sleeping pills and passed away in her bed.

– Were you very sad when she died?

– Both yes and no. The grief was mixed with relief, I must admit. She hadn't felt really well in thirty years.

– Did she manage to take care of mamma then?

– No, she wasn't up to much. Periodically it went well, but quite often it was I who had to take over. Sometimes we got help from a neighbour wife.

– How did mamma react when grandma died?

– I don't remember it very well. Hasn't she told you anything? You may ask her if you want to know, because we haven't talked much about it. Barbro and I were very young when she was born, and in addition to Barbro's recurrent depressions, your mother actually didn't get a particularly good childhood.

Grandma took her own life. I was only five years old when it happened. I knew she was sick and had to go to the hospital from time to time to get help, so sometimes she wasn't home. At last, she just disappeared and was never there again when I came to grandpa to be looked after. I don't remember how he explained it to me. I didn't miss her very much, because it was grandpa who had taken care of me all the time, and he went on doing so after her death as well. There was no major difference for me, and I soon forgot about her.

I understand that mamma is the way she is because of grandma, but that makes no difference to me. I needed what I needed all the same and was hurt by not getting it.

You get hurt without knowing it. You grow up with it and are shaped by it to fit in and not be a nuisance. You abandon yourself and become different from who you are. Others may see that you are damaged, but no one cares. Eventually you discover it yourself and begin to feel ashamed.

PART FIVE

Petra has broken up with her boyfriend in Germany and moved back to Sweden again. She called today and told me. She will be living with her father for a while now while she is looking for a job and a flat.

She suggested we would go out to eat on Saturday. "We can go to Luckan on Vaksalagatan," she said. "That's where Helmut and I met."

"Was it?" I said. "I didn't know that. But we can eat at my place instead. I have moved and live alone now."

"What? Have you dumped Bernt?"

"No, it was he who dumped me," I said.

Almost the first thing I thought when we had hung up was if I could tell her about the rape. Before, I probably would have done it, but now I don't know. We haven't met in over two years. We corresponded for a while, but it ended soon, and since then we haven't had contact.

We have been best friends since we went to high school. We are quite different in our manners, but we have always got along well. She is lively and talkative, and I am calm and quiet. We are different in appearance as well. She is big and dark, I am small and light, and she has short hair and I have long.

I wonder what happened between her and Helmut. She will tell me, if I know her at all. And she will ask why I am not together with Bernt any longer. What should I answer to that? That I discovered he was a potential rapist?

All men are potential rapists.

That doesn't mean that every man walks around and has the desire to rape, and would do so if given the opportunity, or that he refrains for fear of getting caught. This means that it isn't possible to tell by a man's appearance whether he is dangerous or not, but that a woman must be prepared that he *can* be. I have learned that. All women are potential rape victims, and all men are potential rapists.

Bernt almost did it. He was more than potential. He had a barrier to the decisive step, but how long would that barrier have lasted if he had become sufficiently aroused and angry?

Should I tell Petra what he did? I haven't told Göran, but maybe she, who knows him, should know?

And should I tell her about the rape or not? I should be able to stand on a stage and tell it to the whole world. But just because you *can*, you may not *want* to.

I won't tell her.

Should I tell her about Göran, then?

Yes, I should. After all, we are together now.

She has met him once, but she may not remember it. It was at work, when she came and picked me up because we were going to her place, and then I introduced her to him.

I have missed her. It's going to be fun to meet her again. I said she could bring a bottle of wine if she wanted, and she would, she said. We can drink and talk shit about our exes and revive old memories. I only have to pay attention to myself so that I don't lose control and reveal too much.

Petra was the same as ever. It felt like she hasn't been away at all. We became rather tipsy and sat and talked far into the night. I told her about Bernt and Göran, but I didn't mention the rape. I don't really know why. I might do it later when we have met a few more times. Or I don't know. When she talked about her sister, who has also been raped, she was so upset that it might be best if I don't burden her with more of that kind. We also talked about love relationships, and she told me about herself and Helmut, which I knew she would.

– So, it's over between you and Bernt now?
  – Yes.
  – What happened?
  – He just got tired of me.
  – Did he meet another?
  – No, I don't think so. And we were completely agreed that I would move.
  – Yes, wasn't he a bit tricky, to be honest?
  – Yes. It was good that it ended.
  – You were probably too young when you started

being together with him. You need to gain some experi-
ence before committing, because otherwise you haven't
anything to compare with. And how do you know what
love is? Before Helmut, I was in love with a lot of differ-
ent guys, as you know. So incredibly in love that I could
neither eat nor sleep and just wanted to be with HIM all
the time. The rest of the world disappeared as if in a haze
and only he and I existed. One moment I was extremely
happy and the next I felt almost sick. And every time I
hoped and believed I had met the RIGHT MAN and that
it would last forever. But it never did. Sometimes it only
lasted a few days, sometimes until we had had sex, some-
times a little longer. There are those who believe that the
closest you can get to another person is to have sex. As
if you would know each other better after that. But if
you aren't in love before, you won't be afterwards either.
That's my experience in any case. Eventually, I always
woke up and couldn't understand what I had been do-
ing. And when it ended, I was depressed for a while, but
it wasn't the guy I missed the most but that of not being
alone and being horny and feeling beautiful and longed
for and desirable. Yes, you know how I went on. Then I
met Helmut, and it started as it always does, that it felt
exciting and new, and that we lay awake at night talk-
ing and fucking alternately and questioning each other
and telling each other about our lives and our exes and
getting a little jealous. I recognized the pattern very
well, and I thought it wouldn't last with him either. But
it did. Until now, that is. But we'll take that later. How
long have you been single now? It must feel unusual to

you who have never been.

– Since this summer. Though I'm not single any-more.

– What! Have you already met another?

– Yes, but I knew him before. He is a guy at work. You have met him.

– Have I?

– Yes, once when you got there and picked me up when we were going to your place after work.

– You mean that dark, good-looking guy with such incredibly blue eyes? Is he the one you're together with now?

– Yes, Göran.

– Oh, my God! How did it happen? That you got to-gether, I mean. Because you weren't at that time, were you? Were you unfaithful to Bernt with him?

– No, nothing happened until it was over between us.

– But how did it start? First you walked around and worked together for several years, and then all of a sud-den it just said click?

– Yes, something like that. But now you get to tell me about Helmut.

– Yes, as I said on the phone, we met at Luckan, that restaurant on Vaksalagatan, you know. I thought I had told you. We… What is it?

– No, it's nothing. I may have forgotten you told me.

– Yes, but that doesn't matter, you know. Never mind that! I fell in love anyway and was ready to follow him to the end of the world. You know how I was. I did noth-ing but talk about him. And you listened as usual, as

you always have ever since we went to school. Then I skipped you and ran away with him. That's all the thanks you got! Were you very sad?

– No, I was used to you disappearing into your relationships. And deep down, I thought you would come back. It only took a little longer than usual. But for your sake, of course, I hoped it would last.

– Yes, but I say like you, that it was good that it ended. Tell me what he did, Bernt, more than rape you with vegetables.

– Haven't you forgotten about that yet?

– Nope. "Mister Cucumber is dancing here, both waltz and mazurka!" No, sorry, that's nothing to joke about.

– It's okay. But it was only once, and I didn't stop him.

– Why didn't you say no, then? Because you felt guilty that you didn't want to fulfil your so-called marital duties?

– I don't know.

– I know it must be a cock that is pushed into the girl's mouth or vagina for it to be counted as a rape according to the rules, but I don't see it that way. And it shouldn't depend on whether the girl offers resistance or not when she is subjected to physical abuse. It doesn't matter if she is drunk, drugged, unconscious, dead scared or just generally faint-hearted! No one has the right to insult and humiliate her no matter how passive she is! Don't you agree?

– Yes, I do.

– Compare with a robbery. Some robbery victims are struggling and fighting to not lose their bag, some will be knocked down and defenceless, and some hand over the bag without the robber having to do much more than stare threateningly and demand to get it. But robbery it is, nevertheless. The robber commits a crime, and how the victim behaves has nothing to do with it! But when it comes to sex crimes, it's the victim's behaviour that determines if it IS even a crime. It's so fucking wrong! Imagine how many women abusers that walk around out there and think they have every right to treat girls like shit just because the law isn't stricter!

– Mm.

– I know it wouldn't help to tighten up the law, but it would at least feel better if you as a girl had support from it. When a rapist is on trial, it may be presented that he has committed rape before and has a criminal record, which is relevant in that situation. But at the same time, it's presented that the raped girl has dressed defiantly, got drunk at parties, and has had sex with guys before. That's made to be HER criminal record, which will show what an immoral and unreliable person she is. But what she has done isn't CRIMINAL!

– No.

– Explain to me how one can suspect a girl of making false rape allegations against a guy she barely knows! A victim of robbery or assault wouldn't be suspected of that. Not for participation either. "Maybe you gave the wrong signals? Maybe you didn't make it clear enough that you wanted to keep your bag? Maybe you walked *around with the bag in a way that indicated that you wanted to get rid of it? Maybe you invited to it so that he was deceived and couldn't control his desire to take the bag away from you? Maybe you showed signs of WANTING to be knocked down and robbed? Maybe you have been robbed and beaten before, so you didn't mind it happening again?" Yes, you get it, don't you? Such questions are not asked to any other crime victims than sexual crime victims. That's how it turned out for my sister, that she was totally questioned both when she reported the crime to the police and during the trial. You may be glad you haven't experienced something like that anyway! But now I won't preach anymore. Bernt was perhaps okay in his own way, but you still must agree that he had a rather rotten view of women?*

– Yes, he probably had.

– Now you look so strange again. I'm not condemning you for letting him do it, you know!

– No, but that's when I discovered how he was. And additionally, that I didn't trust him.

– Yes, you threw away all your youth on him!

– What was it that made you tired of Helmut, then?

– At first, I was obsessed. I was constantly horny and thought about getting laid all the time, whether he was there or not. Just the thought of him set me going. I couldn't control it and was like a victim of my own lusts, if you know what I mean. It was bloody trying and super wonderful at the same time. But no one can stand having it like that in the long run, and after a while it calmed down for both him and me. For it had

been the same for him. And then, when it has gone so far that you start to cool down, the question is whether there is enough left to build on or not. In the beginning, you're completely fucking blind and see no negative sides at all in each other. But when you've moved together and everyday life begins, all differences and weaknesses emerge slowly but surely. That's what's happened to Helmut and me. I discovered that we didn't fit together. It took a while before I could admit it to myself, because it felt like a great defeat after everything I had sacrificed for his sake. Or not sacrificed perhaps but left. Work, flat, friends, and family... I left my whole fucking NATIVE COUNTRY for his sake! But it simply didn't work, and in the end, I had to face the consequences. So here I am, back as if nothing has happened! I haven't learned anything either, which I can benefit from in the future. I'll make the same damn mistake over again, I guess. But what about you and Göran, then? Are you two still in the passion phase?

– Yes, we probably are.

– It's going to be fun to meet him. Because I can do that, right?

– Yes, of course.

– Are you considering moving together?

– No, we haven't talked about it yet.

– No, since you work together you may meet enough anyway. You also need some space for yourself. Otherwise, you can easily get lost. It's when you're alone that you come to what you feel deep down. And you must not suffocate each other. Listen to the experienced rela-

tionship expert now! But you can probably handle it much better than I did.

– No, but now I'll read to you how to be able to cope with a mature love relationship. It says in a book I have, and which I have recently read. Wait, listen to this. Here it is. If only I could find it... Yes, here it is. This is what it says: "To live in a relationship and still remain true to oneself". Then you should be so that you know what you feel, mean, think and want... and you should take responsibility for your words, promises and actions... and you should have left the child role behind and not constantly demand protection, care, and love. That's what it says. I misread a little, but that's about what it says. Sorry it got a bit slurred.

– It's okay. But for it to work, both must be equally mature, and how big is the chance of that? Eh? The problem is that you never find your equal! In any case, Helmutti wasn't my equal.

– Helmutti? Did you call him that?

– No, I only do it now when I talk about him. Mutti, you know. He needed a mother. He wasn't as mature as I thought. I wasn't either, but more than him anyway. When the fucking passion had ended and I saw what he was like, I felt superior to him. It's not a good feeling to have in a relationship. You want it to feel equal.

– Yes, it also happened to me with Bernt, that I started looking down on him. But how long were you in that passion, then? Wait, I saw that there was something about it in the book.

– About six months. If I had waited a little longer, I

would never have gone with him to Germany. Because then the truth began to emerge. Have you found it?

— Yes, here it is. "How long does a passion last?" it says. According to a study that has been done a passion lasts for about a year. After about three years, one percent of the couples in the study were capable of passion, in thirty-three percent the passion had turned to tenderness, in fifty percent to indifference, habit and rut, and in sixteen percent to negative emotions such as aggression, disgust and hatred.

— Yes, you can be so fucking blind, so that what begins in ecstasy and tremendous happiness ends in disgust and hatred! Hope you and Göran do better than we did.

— Yes, I hope so too. But you get a little scared if there is only a thirty percent chance.

— Yes, I don't understand why it never lasts for me. What am I doing wrong? Do you remember when we were out dancing? Then I still had hope of meeting Mister Right. I almost no longer have that hope. The only right one simply doesn't exist. Or what do you think? Is Göran the only right one for you?

— Yes, I think so. But probably everyone thinks so in the beginning, so it can change, I suppose.

Petra has also felt obsessed and like a victim of her lusts, so I am not alone. I don't have to feel abnormal. But I didn't tell her that I feel that way. I didn't tell her about the rape either. But she was very observant and noticed that I reacted to certain things she said. When she mentioned Lucullus, and when she talked about rape victims, she saw in my face that I was unpleasantly affected. But she misinterpreted it, and I didn't correct her.

It was fun to meet her again. I am enlivened by her way of behaving. She talks a lot, but she is curious and interested in others and not as mamma, who only thinks of herself and can't listen at all. Petra says anything that comes into her head and doesn't care what others may think about it. She is much more open and much braver than me.

I wonder what Göran would think of her. I am going to ask him if he remembers her from the time I introduced her to him.

What will I think of *his* friends, then? He has a couple of mates with whom he plays tennis, but he seldom talks about them and doesn't seem anxious in me meeting them. And what will I think of his parents and brothers? I hope it takes a while before he thinks it's time to introduce me to his family.

Mamma liked Bernt, and she would probably like Göran as well, but what would he think of her? I don't want him to meet her. Not until I have told him what she is like, and how I feel about her myself anyway.

I haven't applied for any courses this autumn. I can't concentrate on studying when I feel like this. Maybe it isn't to continue studying I should do either. Maybe I should get married and have children instead. No, I am not ready for that yet, but I want to know how it will be with Göran and me before I decide what to do later. When the passion is over, there may be nothing left. What if that happens to us? But I was interested in him even before the passion arose, and he was interested in me, and that must mean there is more, I think.

It's not good to doubt. That's what I have decided not to do. And for the most part, I am sure it will last. What Petra and I talked about, and what I have read in a book, that just over thirty percent of all passionate relationships are still okay after three years, made me a little uncertain, but deep down I don't doubt how it will go for us. What we have is so deep and strong that it can't just disappear when the passion is over. We agree that it should continue. That's how it feels anyway. But what if I am wrong?

We have started to have common habits. It's nice to know that he can come with me to my home or I to his after work. It's nice to know that we don't always have to part when the workday is over.

I have become accustomed to waking up beside him and getting up at the same time as him. I have become accustomed to hearing him shower and wash and brush his teeth in the bathroom and to share the kitchen and sit opposite him at the breakfast table.

Petra said that you need to be alone sometimes so as not to lose yourself, and that Göran and I may have a greater need for it, because we meet all day at work as well.

But I think it increases the tension. I see him and hear him, and sometimes when he comes close, I smell his scent, but I am not allowed to touch him. I must keep my distance and pretend like nothing is going on. And he does the same. We continue with it in the car as well, when we are on our way home, so that he can drive properly and not become a danger to other traffic.

In a couple of years, when the passion is over, we may think we meet too much, but now we don't want to be separated at all.

Göran and I are not very keen on talking about ourselves, and therefore I have come up with a little game for us, so that we at least can get the most important things out of us. You can't sit and tell the story of your life in a broad outline. You do this piece by piece, and you leave out certain things and keep them to yourself. I don't think it's right to turn oneself inside out for another person. But there are always things you wonder about and want to know.

One evening when we were lying on his bed I said:

"Now there will be an interrogation!"

"Ah, will it?" he said and sounded amused.

"Yes, after dealing with our worst traumas, it's time for some cold facts now."

"Okay, I'm ready."

"Oh, it won't be easy to stick to cold facts if you are going to use words that make me get…"

"…warm?" he said and smiled.

"Yes, but we may come back to that after the interrogation."

– Full name.

   – Göran Valdemar Zander.

   – Valdemar?

   – Yes, that one I've got from my grandfather.

   – Age?

   – Twenty-nine.

   – What subjects did you like best in school?

   – Gymnastics and mathematics.

   – What did you want to work with as an adult?

   – I didn't really know. Sorry to interrupt, but what are your parents' professions?

   – Mamma is a hairdresser and papa was a high-ranking military officer. Well, he still is, I suppose, but I don't know, because we have no contact. Have you done your military service or were you…

   – …exempted from it or a conscientious objector?

   – Yes.

   – No, I have done my military service.

   – How did you like it in the military?

   – Not so good.

   – What do you remember best from that time?

   – That you were never alone and that everyone saw what you were doing all the time. You were with others around the clock. During the exercises, when you slept, when you woke up, when you ate, washed, showered, went to the loo… There weren't even any doors to the shower cubicles or to the toilets.

   – Wasn't it hard to have it that way?

   – Yes, but it was the same for everyone and not much

to do about it.

– Did you never consider refusing weapons?

– No, I wanted to see what it was like. Get that experience. I joined up without any preconceived notions in order to form my own opinion. But from the beginning, I realized that much of what I had heard about the military was true. It was a hard training, both physically and mentally, with strenuous exercises and unsympathetic officers.

– What did you have to do?

– Well, on several occasions there were for example long exercises without sleep. It was all about trying to stay awake for three days and at the same time solve various tasks during hard physical exertion and with constant relocations. Lying out in the woods in twenty degrees cold without fire. The enemy could see us if we made a fire… Some got hallucinations due to lack of sleep, and some became demobilized because of mental problems for other reasons.

– What else did you do?

– Well, once it was a week of blasting service. A tough commander began by saying: "Good morning fucking recruits, if you make any mistakes this week, I promise to shovel up the remains of you afterwards." While he showed how to prime an explosive cartridge on a fuse, he said that if you adapted it wrong, you had no fingers left afterwards or could even have lost your whole hand.

– That doesn't sound particularly nice.

– No, it wasn't. I should of course have chosen something closer to my interests and my personality. Then it

would probably have gone much better. Instead, I joined a group where I was an outsider, a group where I didn't belong, and where people were annoyed with me because I stood out from the crowd. The fact that a person like me, with a view to studying at university after the service, ended up in a group where the great majority were practically and technically oriented, meant that we didn't have much in common. It became very clear to me that I didn't fit in, and in that situation, you're of course a little extra exposed.

– How? What happened?

– Well, one evening… One evening I happened to fall asleep on my bed on top of the day blanket with my clothes on, and it apparently annoyed the sergeant who inspected the barrack-room that evening, because when I woke up in the middle of the night, I discovered that I was tied. I groped in the dark to find out how I was stuck, and after a while I felt that several straps had been attached to the edges of the bed and tightened over my body. After some fumbling, I got loose, got up and undressed, crawled under the blanket, and fell asleep again. The day after, I was told by the guy who had the bed next to me that it was the sergeant who had strapped me in while I slept.

– What a ridiculous thing to do.

– Mm. I don't mean that I was harassed or frozen out, because that with the straps was just a one-off event, but my period of service wasn't very positive, and I really looked forward to the demob.

It's been ten years now, but when he told me how he experienced his military service, I felt sorry for him. Once he was strapped to his bed by a lousy sergeant just because he had fallen asleep with his clothes on. Another time, in a morning line-up when the sergeant thought he had shaved carelessly, he was asked if he had used a mirror when he shaved, and when he replied that he had done so, the sergeant tried to make fun of him at his expense by saying: "Then, damn it, use a razor instead next time!"

– Isn't it tiresome to have to shave every day?

   – It becomes a habit. Do you like beard?

   – No, I don't. I like beard-stubble, but not beard and moustaches.

   – Aha, you like stubble?

   – Yes, it looks masculine and sexy.

   – Hm. At least now I'm not the one who…

   – No, sorry. How old were you when you first slept with a girl?

   – Sixteen.

   – How old was she?

   – Fifteen.

   – How many girls have you been together with?

   – Three, apart from the current one.

   – Tell me about the first one.

   – The first was called Linda, and I met her on a gask when I was out having fun in a student's club one evening.

– What's a gask?

– It's a three-course dinner with a dress code, you could say. You must be dressed in a certain way. And there are speeches, song, and entertainment. Every club has its own traditional gask.

– Were you very engaged in student life?

– Yes, you can probably say I was. In that environment, I felt much more at home than I had done in the military.

– What was there to do?

– Well, firstly, you can become a member of one or more unions and clubs, and once you have signed up for a club, you have access to them all. Everything at the clubs is run by the students themselves, for the students' own benefit. You can work in the bar, serve at large dinners, or sit on committees of various kinds. And there are lots of associations and organizations to get involved in. It can be choirs, orchestras, sports clubs, and entertainment such as spex, which is a kind of amateur theatre or performance with song and music. There are also lots of different types of dinners. Everything from sexor, which are simpler dinners, to gasker and sumptuous balls. The most famous is the spring ball at the castle in connection with the celebration of the Walpurgis night. Then a formal outfit is required in the form of a tailcoat and long dress.

– Were you at a spring ball?

– Yes, I was there with Linda.

– What did she look like?

– At the ball?

– No, just in general.

– She was small and plump and had medium blonde hair and glasses.

– What made you interested in her?

– Her intellect. No, I don't really know. But there was no great physical attraction between us in any case. Not of the calibre I have experienced recently, and which has…

– Now you have got on to dangerous ground again.

– I have?

– Yes, as an interrogator, I have to make sure I'm cold and objective and not let myself be affected by things I hear.

– And you don't quite succeed in that?

– No, I get so…

– …warm?

– Hm. Yes. How long were you together with Linda?

– For five months.

– Why did it end?

– Well, who knows? Because the conditions were bad from the beginning and because the physical attraction was lacking.

– Yes.

– But that's not the case here, I notice.

– No, now I must probably… Now we must… The interrogation is hereby concluded at eighteen minutes past ten.

PART SIX

When I was growing up, no one listened to me and cared about my feelings. It's too late to redress that now. That Göran listens doesn't make it disappear. It should have been then, when I was little and needed it, and not now, when I am an adult and can do without. It should have been *mamma* and *papa* listening, so I wouldn't have had to feel so alone and invisible. But I knew nothing else and thought it should be that way. If I was sad sometimes, I was told it was wrong. "Whimper" and "self-pity" papa called it, and that was the worst he knew.

When I think of Göran asking questions about my childhood, I feel reluctant, as if I don't trust that he is interested, or it bores me to talk about myself.

Is that the truth, or have I just got used to not doing it so I can't feel that I need it? I know that Göran is interested in me and wants to know how my life has been, but to me it doesn't feel important.

Or am I afraid? If I try to remember what it was

like, I perhaps get sad, and I don't want him to feel sorry for me. Or I just begin to feel sorry for myself, and what's the point of that? If all the grief wells up, it may not be possible to stop it, and if he wants to comfort me, I may not be able to receive it. There is a difference between receiving comfort for a physical injury and for a mental one. Being comforted because you have been the victim of a violent crime is easier than being comforted because no one has cared about you.

I remember thinking once about Göran and me that we perhaps could have sex, but not love. This is what I meant that time, although I didn't understand it. I have opened to him physically but not mentally. Well, I am a little open, and that's what makes me feel sad. But I release it only when I am alone and in small portions. If he would make me open to him in his presence, I might drown and die. I cry just thinking of it and know that I won't let it happen.

I shouldn't have invented the interrogation game that can lead to it. All I can hope is that he will ask the wrong kind of questions so that I don't need to open up more than I want to.

I also asked the wrong kind of questions. But I can't feel that I want to know how his life was when he was little. It doesn't matter what our childhood was like. We have become who we are, and now is now.

I am not sure the grief is due to my childhood. I

am just guessing and trying to get it to fit in somewhere because I don't understand where it comes from. I am tired of it. I am tired of not understanding.

I start crying without knowing why. I sob and curl up and moan. I think of Göran and cry even more. When I admit that he loves me, I must at the same time grieve over that no one has done it before. Now that everything is okay, it becomes extra clear to me how empty and cold my life has been. If I am going to tell him things, at least it won't be about my boring papa or my self-absorbed mamma. *He loves me and you don't, so you can just go to hell!*

Once upon a time, I loved and needed both mamma and papa and hoped I would get love back. I thought for a long time that mamma cared about me although she had difficulty showing it. I thought that if I gave her space, she would give me space in return. But she didn't. She hasn't done that. To the very last, I have struggled to get room to exist, but now it's over. Now I know the truth and don't have to try anymore.

It's not often that Göran and I drink wine, but one evening when we did, I overcame my resistance and said he could interrogate me if he wanted to. There was a small break in the middle, but then we went on.

– Name?

– Eva Susanne Holmkvist.

– Age?

– Twenty-four.

– Occupation? No, you don't have to answer that. I don't know, but it doesn't feel quite okay to questioning like this.

– You don't have to do it if you don't want to.

– Yes, I want to, but…

– It's my fault that it doesn't feel okay

– It is?

– Yes, I feel resistance to it, even though I want you to do it.

– Why is that?

– I don't know.

– Should I quit, then?

– No, that's not fair.

– It doesn't have to be.

– Yes, I think so.

– If I ask things you don't want to answer, you can just say "pass" or "no comment".

– But I think I should be able to answer everything, as you did. And it's me who has come up with the idea that we should do this.

– Hold interrogations.

– Mm.

– And I'm a skilled interrogator, I've been told.

– Yes, maybe that's why I'm afraid.

– Afraid that I'll draw all your secrets out of you?

– I have no secrets. No important ones anyway.

– What are you afraid of, then?

– That I'll be sad. I am already sad.

– Mm. What are you sad about?

– I get sad when you respect me and listen to me and understand me. Since that's the right thing to do and no one has done it before.

He understood my resistance and made me start talking about how I felt instead. Before the acquisition of "cold facts" had even initiated properly, I began to cry. He does what mamma and papa should have done but didn't do. He is interested and listens and understands. He loves me. Sometimes I can hardly bear it. Why can't I be normal and just receive it? I don't want him to have trouble with me. When that happens, I am ashamed and feel bad and stupid. I want it to be easy and uncomplicated, as it's meant to be. There is no point in me trying to pretend either, because he notices. He notices when I am closed. Only the truth is useable.

– Now you can go on asking.

– Okay. What were you afraid of when you were little?

– Fire. That it would start burning in the house where we lived.

– Did you live in the country or in the city?

– In the city.

– Did you have many playmates?

– No, almost none at all. Before I started school, we moved several times because of papa's work, but then I had a best friend in class.

– Which school subjects did you like best?

– Drawing, math and Swedish.

– What profession did you want when you grew up?

– I wanted to be a journalist, like grandpa.

– How did you behave as a child?

– With adults, I was quiet and shy. With my friend, I was rather dominant at times. How was your way?

– With adults I was precious, and at school I was a dry little swot.

– Dry?

– Yes, you were called that when you weren't interested in girls. What about guys, then?

– When I was ten, I was in love with a guy named

Peter. We were together and kissed behind the tool shed and things like that.

— How old were you the first time you slept with a guy?

— Sixteen. It was with Bernt, and I haven't slept with anyone else until now, with you. I should never have done it with him.

— Why not?

— Because I didn't want to.

— Weren't you in love with him?

— No, I wasn't, but I didn't understand that. And I didn't feel any physical attraction to him. When he had sex with me, it just felt forced and wrong. I didn't want to. My body didn't want to. I shouldn't have let it happen.

— Why were you together with him, then?

— To avoid being alone, I think. He was caring and kind, and I needed that. In return, he could sleep with me.

— You were bartering?

— Yes, we were. And now I want you to… want what I felt at that time to be… driven away.

— Driven away? Yes, okay, I think we should be able to arrange that…

It turned out as it always does, and I can hear Petra's voice when she said: *We lay awake at night talking and fucking alternately.*

But Göran and I don't fuck. I don't call it that. Nor do I call it to make love, because that makes it sound like we don't *always* love. I don't call it anything, and neither does he. We only do it because we can't resist it.

Afterwards, the interrogation continued.

– What happened between you and Bernt after the rape? You hinted he had difficulty dealing with it?

– Yes, he became very strange.

– How?

– He got mad at me.

– Mad? Did he get mad *at you? How could he be so callous?*

– I don't know. But I already knew when I was at the police station that I wouldn't be able to tell him.

– Why couldn't you?

– I don't know. I felt that he…

– You once said he was "the same". What did you mean by that?

– How can you remember I said that?

– I have a good memory. But what did you mean?

– It felt like he could also rape.

– Rape you?

– Yes, or at least get the urge to do so, if he felt rejected and angry. He didn't care about my feelings. But I didn't do it myself either, because I let him sleep with me even though I didn't want to.

– In what way did he become strange?

– He became hostile and scornful and seemed to think I had agreed to it.

– Agreed to be raped?

– Yes. And I interpreted it as him linking it to what I let him do.

– What did you let him do?

– Sleep with me even though I didn't want to.

– Nothing else?

– Well… yes.

I don't want to lie to him, and when he asks out of genuine interest, it's difficult for me not to answer, even though I may have a feeling in which way things are going. He makes me tell him more than I have intended to, and I don't know if it's good or not. He asked me about Bernt, and I had difficulty getting it all out. But why should I feel complicit in what he did? Why should I be ashamed of it? Why should I protect him by keeping quiet about it?

He didn't force me. I let him do it. Am I not an accessory, then? Yes, I think I am.

Petra wanted to call it rape, although it isn't according to the law. But how can it be? He didn't force me, and he didn't hurt me. No matter how hard I try, I can't make myself an innocent victim of it.

It wasn't easy for me to tell Göran, but I did because he asked, and I couldn't bring myself to lie or reject him by refusing to answer.

"What else?" he said.

"I let him tuck a cucumber in me."

It went completely quiet when I had said it. He doesn't understand, I thought, and I can't expect him to, when I don't even understand it myself. I didn't know how to proceed when he just kept quiet. Now he is put to the test again, I thought, and this he won't be able to handle. I thought he would question me and think that what I had done was incomprehensible and condemn me. Instead, he took sides with me and made me see it from a different angle. He helped me make it understandable.

– Why do you think he wanted to do such a thing? Did he explain it?
    – No.
    – Maybe it was because he felt inadequate?
    – Yes, and that was my fault.
    – How could it be your fault?
    – Because I slept with him though I had no desire. He must have noticed.
    – The barter didn't work properly?
    – No, and I thought there was something wrong with me, and he thought it was him who wasn't good enough, just because we were together for the wrong reasons.
    – Mm. How did you feel when he did it?
    – Physically, you mean?
    – No, not physically.
    – I didn't feel anything. Not physically either, if he had expected me to. I know I was humiliated, but it didn't feel that way. I may have thought he was perfectly within his rights because I wasn't honest with him.
    – Mm.

– How come that you always know what's the right thing to say? That you always ask the right kind of questions so I can't refrain answering?

– Could it be due to my excellent interrogation technique?

– No, it's because you understand. How come you always understand?

– I don't.

– Yes, you do. You understand everything, and so you make me understand too, so that I can explain to both you and myself. I think it's fantas... fan-tas-tic. *Is it called that? It sounds so strange.*

– Yes, that's what it's called.

– Yes. And now I can barely remember what I have said. But it doesn't matter, because now I know that you know, and next time it's my turn to interrogate, and then I'll ask you about…

– …my innermost secrets?

– Yes, I'll ask you about that, but you don't have to answer if you don't want to.

When we drink wine, I become tipsy and start chattering right away, but on Göran it's barely noticeable. I feel stupid when I understand that he has better check on me than I have myself, and that he seems amused by how I behave when I am affected.

– Don't you feel the wine at all? Am I the only one who becomes like this?

– Yes, I feel a little. But there are biological differences between women and men that cause that the same amount of alcohol gives different ethanol concentrations in the blood. The female body contains less water than the male body, and that makes the alcohol concentration higher in women. Women also have less of the enzyme that breaks down alcohol in the body than men have.

– Yes, I knew there was a difference, but I didn't know exactly what it's due to. How come you know it so well?

– It's because I once found out properly and still remember it.

– Why did you do that?

– Because I wondered why my mother always got so awkward at parties when father didn't.

– How old were you then?

– Twelve, thirteen years. I went to the library and looked it up, and since then I remember it.

– Did your mother drink often?

– No, she didn't. It was just me who tended to be ashamed of her when she didn't behave as she used to. When I was that age, that is.

– Did it help that you found out what it was due to?

– Yes, it did, because then I could think that she couldn't help it.

– Do you think the same about me now that you notice that I'm more affected than you?

– I'm not exactly thinking it, but I'm aware that's how it is.

– How much would you need to drink then, to be as affected as I am by this wine?

– I don't know. And it's not that I don't feel it.

– Was your mother kind?

– Yes, she was.

– Mine wasn't. Isn't.

– No?

– I just want to tell you so that you understand why you haven't got to meet her. Do you want *to meet her?*

– No, I have no need for that unless you want me to.

– No, I don't want you to.

– Are you mad at her?

– Yes.

– Why?

– Because she never listens.

I talked about mamma, and when I think of her now, a wave of anger wells up in me. *Why the hell aren't you listening to me, fucking bitch!*

But the worst thing wasn't that she didn't listen, but that she talked all the time, so I got no room for my own thoughts. She *raped* and *invaded* me with her fucking talk! She may do all the talking because no one listened to *her* when she was little, but I don't give a damn, because she had no right to do as she did to me anyway! She would have shut up and left me alone!

I haven't told Göran yet how difficult it has been for me with her. How could he understand how it feels to never have space for oneself together with the person you want to reach and need? Well, maybe he would understand. But I would only feel immature and fastidious if I started complaining about her.

PART SEVEN

Previously, I thought that when grandpa dies, and I am not allowed to stay in his apartment any longer, I can move to Göran instead. But now that I own the apartment and imagine we are moving in together I am not sure I want to. I want to feel free and independent in relation to him, so that he doesn't lose respect for me. I don't want the tension between us to disappear, and perhaps it would if we were always together.

The excitement also arises at work, where we don't show what we feel and can't do everything we want. I enjoy postponing it and having to wait. When I think that way, I feel that that's the right thing to do and that that's how he also wants it.

Everything is okay now, but the sorrow isn't gone. I have tried to feel, and I have tried to guess what it may be due to, and why there are no words for it, and now I begin to understand that it comes from the fact that I have always been so alone. I haven't understood what emotional seclusion and loneliness I lived in when I was little. I didn't even have myself. I had to give up and abandon myself in order to survive.

Everything I think about makes me cry. Everything feels so sad. I lie on my bed and close my eyes, and when I open them the tears well up and run down my temples and into my ears.

What did Göran once say? That mental pain heals if only you can endure the suffering. That's what he said, and I know it's true. But when will it end?

Sometimes I feel inferior to him. When he told me about the university, for example, I realized how inexperienced I am compared to him, and how much more than he I need. I don't ask for it, but I get it anyway, and I don't know what to give him in return.

He said that Bernt and I were bartering, but what about him and me, then? I am afraid he might think I am childish and immature and have nothing but my body to give him. I have shown childish feelings to him, but he has never shown childish feelings to me. Doesn't he have any, or does he control himself?

Göran wasn't home, and I had started cooking dinner. When I took a cucumber out of the fridge and was about to cut it into slices, I suddenly got angry and threw it across the floor and started crying. *You stupid fucking shit!* I shouted soundlessly to Bernt. *I don't want this! I don't want to!*

It wasn't the whole truth Göran and I reached

when we understood what Bernt was doing. The rest of the truth is that I didn't want the fucking cucumber to be pushed into me! He had no right to do that to me no matter how much we bartered! Petra was right when she called it rape. How could I be so stupid that I couldn't feel what his action meant? It didn't matter that I was passive and let it happen! It was still just as wrong!

I don't have to tell Göran. What I felt I was shouting to Bernt was between him and me. It's enough that I know it myself. And what I felt I was shouting to mamma was between her and me. Göran doesn't need to know exactly what happens when I free myself and realize the truth. He just needs to feel that I become stronger and freer with time. And I know he senses it. Every time it happens, he notices it, and every time he is there and receives me.

I am grateful he is waiting for me, but it doesn't feel right that he has to do it just because I am so tardy. I don't want him to be like a parent who follows and waits for his child's development and maturity, and I, for my part, don't want to be like a child. I want us both to be adults and equal.

When he got home and opened the refrigerator door, he noticed that a part of the cucumber was missing.

"Where did the rest of the cucumber go, then?" he said.

"I threw it on the floor so it died," I said.

"Good," he said, and I knew without him need-
ing to explain it, that he understood what it meant.

Göran and I have continued with the interrogation game, and I have told him about my teens. That I was the good and quiet girl who got good grades and was a lot by myself and didn't have many friends. In high school, I had one best friend who I hung out with both at school and in my free time. We had coffee and went to the cinema and baby-sat sometimes. When I was alone at home I read, drew, painted, and listened to music.

And Göran has told me about his exes Anna and Therese. It was he who broke up with Anna, and Therese who broke up with him. About Anna he said she was "unbalanced and labile", and about Therese he said that their relationship ended due to "short but lasting disagreement". When I asked in what way Anna was unbalanced, he said: "It doesn't matter anymore." But I wanted to know and tried to get him to continue.

– Don't you want to talk about her?
   – I don't know.
   – Couldn't she accept that you broke up?

– Yes, that's right. How did you know?

– I'm just guessing. What did she do?

– Yes, that's what was so... unpleasant.

– What happened?

– She... I was surprised when she reacted so strongly, because I had thought she felt about the same as I did, that we didn't have much in common and that it would soon end.

– But that wasn't the case?

– Well, objectively it was, but she evidently couldn't accept it. Or if she didn't experience it that way. I don't know.

– How did she react?

– She became hysterical and said she couldn't live without me. I hadn't had the slightest idea that she felt that way, and that says a lot about how bad it was...

– How long had you been together?

– For five months.

– Did she threaten to commit suicide?

– No, not really. At first, she begged and begged us to continue, and then she said I would regret leaving her, but I didn't know what she meant by that.

– How did it feel when she reacted the way she did?

– I had difficulty grasping it, because she hadn't seemed particularly committed towards the end.

– Maybe it was just being rejected she couldn't stand?

– Yes, that's how it might have been, because then... No, it's just as well I show you. This was while I was studying, and I had started working as a taxi driver *during evenings and nights to earn a little extra, and that's what became important in connection with her.*

He fetched a binder and looked for some papers in it which he removed and let me read. It was a district court judgement. I got ready to cry when I read it, because I understood immediately that what was written in it wasn't true. The allegations that had led to the trial were false. No one must do this to him! I thought. He isn't the one who did this!

In connection with driving a taxi, Göran Zander has harassed Pernilla Hägg and Carina Sundgren in a way that could be expected to violate Pernilla Hägg's and Carina Sundgren's sexual integrity, by asking questions with a sexual meaning such as how often they masturbate, how they usually do when they masturbate, if they have any sex toys, what sex position they like best, if they want to sleep with him and the like. This took place on 17 May 1987 during a taxi ride between Västra Ågatan 14, Uppsala and Brunna, Uppsala municipality.
Göran Zander committed the act with intent.
LAW: 6 Chapter 10 § 2 paragraph of the Criminal Code

Pernilla Hägg has requested Göran Zander to pay damages to her with 4 000 plus interest from the date of the crime until full payment is made. The amount refers to violation.

Carina Sundgren has requested Göran Zander to pay damages to her with 7 000 plus interest from the date of the crime until full payment is made. The amount refers to violation.

Göran Zander has denied the crime and opposed paying any damages to Carina Sundgren and Pernilla Hägg.

THE INVESTIGATION
Interrogations have been held with Pernilla Hägg, Carina Sundgren and Göran Zander. In addition the prosecutor has relied on evidence in the form of information from Uppsala Taxi and evidence from a photo confrontation. The persons heard have mainly stated the following.

Pernilla Hägg
She had been to a pub that night. Shortly after one o'clock at night, she left the pub to take a taxi home with her friend Carina Sundgren. They jumped into a taxi and went towards Brunna where they both live. She was sitting in the back seat of the taxi and Carina Sundgren was sitting in the front seat next to the driver. The driver asked them where their boyfriends were. The driver then asked many questions with a sexual meaning, such as how often they masturbate, what they usually do when they masturbate and if they have any sex toys. She tried to turn the conversation onto something else. The taxi ride took about twenty minutes. She got out of the

taxi at her home while Carina Sundgren went on to her home. She recognizes Göran Zander in the courtroom and is absolutely certain that he is the perpetrator.

Carina Sundgren
She and her friend Pernilla Hägg took a taxi to go home from a pub. It was about one o'clock at night. The driver started asking nasty questions, such as if she had a dildo, if she usually uses it and if she usually masturbates. The questions were directed at both her and Pernilla Hägg. The atmosphere was stiff. She was scared and laughed away most of it. After about twenty minutes' drive the taxi stopped outside Pernilla Hägg's housing and Pernilla Hägg got out of the taxi. She herself did not get out of the taxi with Pernilla Hägg because she lives a short distance away and because she didn't think anything more would happen. The driver's statements became more intense when Pernilla Hägg had left the taxi. The driver said that he wanted to come with her home, but she said no. She did not want the driver to find out where she lived, so she gave an address a little further away. When the taxi stopped at that address, the driver said that he wanted to come home with her and that it was no problem for him that she had a boyfriend.

Göran Zander
He admits that Pernilla Hägg and Carina Sundgren went in his taxi that evening, as it emerged from the written evidence. He often picks up customers at the place where the plaintiffs stated that they stepped into

his taxi. However, he does not remember the current driving and has no memory of Pernilla Hägg and Carina Sundgren. He has never spoken in the manner claimed by the plaintiffs.

REASONS FOR JUDGMENT
For a conviction in a criminal case, it is required that the court, through the investigation that has been presented, finds it beyond reasonable doubt that the accused has committed what the prosecutor claims. A credible statement from the plaintiffs may, in conjunction with what has otherwise emerged in the case, be sufficient for a conviction. The district court initially states that the plaintiffs Pernilla Hägg and Carina Sundgren have a unanimous account of what happened in the taxi that evening and what Göran Zander said during the taxi ride. However, their story contains certain circumstances that give reason to question its credibility and reliability. One such circumstance is that Carina Sundgren, despite stating that she felt scared, didn't leave the taxi at the same time as Pernilla Hägg but continued alone with Göran Zander. This will give the court cause to question whether, in case Göran Zander has asked questions with sexual focus, these questions have been intended to arouse discomfort or otherwise harass the plaintiffs in the manner required for the issues to be assessed as sexual harassment. Göran Zander has stated that he does not remember the current driving but that he would never speak in the way alleged by the prosecutor. In an overall assessment of the in-

vestigation that has been presented, the district court assesses that there is a reasonable doubt as to whether Göran Zander was really guilty of the crime of sexual harassment. The prosecution must therefore be dismissed.

Since Göran Zander is not convicted of the crime, he will also not pay damages to the plaintiffs.

Dissenting opinion
Former chief judge in district court Erik Westergren and lay assessor Eivor Johansson are dissentient and have stated the following.

Göran Zander is to be convicted of sexual harassment. The reasons for this are as follows.

Pernilla Hägg's and Carina Sundgren's stories are credible and reliable. They have in a coherent way told how they received many questions with a sexual orientation from Göran Zander, in a way that caused them discomfort. There is no reason to question their stories and there has been no reason why Pernilla Hägg and Carina Sundgren would like to accuse Göran Zander of something he did not do. What Göran Zander has told does not detract from the value of Pernilla Hägg's and Carina Sundgren's stories, as he has not been able to account for what took place in the taxi. All in all, it can be considered that there is no reasonable doubt that Göran Zander stated himself in the ways that the

While studying, he worked at the same time as a taxi driver, and two female passengers, who had been travelling with him at the same occasion, had reported him to the police for sexual harassment. It was completely absurd. But I didn't understand what it had to do with Anna. When it happened, he also didn't understand why two girls, completely unknown to him, lied and reported him to the police. It wasn't until much later the thought struck him that it could be Anna who was behind it. It turned out that she was acquainted with one of the girls, and that that girl, whose name was Carina, owed her a lot of money and wouldn't have to repay it if she did Anna a favour instead. He found out when he looked up Carina's friend, who told him that Anna had hired Carina to take revenge on him and that Carina had taken her friend with her so as not to have to do it on her own. Anna had told Carina that Göran had raped her but that she couldn't prove it and that's why she wanted revenge.

– *Did you put Anna against the wall later?*

– No, then she was no longer at the university, and I didn't bother to look for her. Didn't want to either.

– How did you feel when you found out the truth?

– That it was damn nasty of her, and that I was glad I had been acquitted. Not everyone in court thought I would be.

– But it wasn't your fault that it didn't last with Anna. And it wasn't your fault that you and Jenny were hit. But both times the guilty one got away.

– Yes, that's how it is.

– What do you think about it?

– If I think I should have been more persistent to see that justice was done?

– No, it wasn't worth trying, I suppose.

– No, I didn't think so. Or maybe I should have believed I was meant to suffer misery?

– No, did you think so?

– No, not exactly. I may have done it right then, when Jenny had died, but I understand that it was just a coincidence.

– Mm. Did you never meet Anna again?

– No, I didn't.

– She must have been mentally ill in some way if she could do as she did to you.

– Yes, she probably was.

– It was so unfair! You would never go on like those girls claimed you did! You who are so… decent.

I started crying out of compassion for him and because everything was so unfair. It just welled up in me, and I couldn't stop it.

– Sorry, I didn't mean to upset you.

– No, don't worry about it. Had you started working for Egon when the trial took place?

– No, it was in the spring, almost a year later, and I didn't start working there until the autumn.

– Did any of your acquaintances doubt that you were innocent?

– I don't know. Not many of them were told that it had happened. I did like you, that I kept rather quiet about it.

– Why?

– Yes, why… Because I couldn't explain it, I think. From the beginning, I didn't connect it at all with Anna. It was completely incomprehensible to me before I knew how it was connected. Why would two unknown girls want to run me in like that for no reason, many would surely have thought and maybe doubted that I was innocent.

– What did you think about it yourself?

– I pondered it quite a lot, and the only thing I came to was that I must have been mixed up with another driver and another taxi ride on another occasion. It took a while before we were questioned by the police, and I had no clear memory of that driving.

– Didn't you remember any girls at all?

– Yes, faintly. But I didn't say that to the police or at the trial.

– Why not?

– I had a faint memory of driving a couple of girls who talked a lot about sex and tried to shock and provoke me, but if I mentioned it, it might just seem like I was trying to put the blame on them instead, I thought.

– Mm.

– And I didn't remember if it was exactly those two girls I had driven out to Brunna, or if there were some others. I didn't remember any exact words either, since I had a habit of never listening to drunken talk.

– So, they were drunk?

– Yes, and I didn't mention that to the police either.

– Is it a punishable offense to lie to the police?

– No, you have the right to do so. Keep silent, leave out, or lie.

– Oh, I didn't know that.

– Yes, that's how it is. What was it about when it came to you?

He also withheld things from the police. He did as I did. And he remembered that I once said that I lied to the police after the rape. He asked what it was, and I told him. It wasn't at all difficult now that he knows so much else about me and I know that he has done almost the same thing himself.

That Göran told me about Anna, and what she subjected him to, has made it feel more equal between us. And in the middle of all the sadness, I was pleased when it turned out that he had thought just like me, that he didn't want to tell the police everything so as not to cause inconvenience and maybe make it worse for himself.

It hurts when I see him in front of me sitting there in the courtroom and being singled out and accused of things he hasn't done. He was only twenty-three years old at that time. He was as old as I was when I had to attend the rape trial.

Göran isn't here and I am lying in bed thinking about him. My neck below my ears feels naked and empty. This is where his face should be. This is where I should feel his mouth and breath and prickly chin against my skin. My skin and my breasts long for his touch. My arms long to hold him.

When he is inside me, I feel protected. It feels warm and safe and… *mutual.* I want to feel him as close to me as possible. It's like I can't get enough of him. I can't get him close enough and not deep enough inside me.

How can it feel so natural and easy with him, as if there are no obstacles at all? He gives me no sense of intrusion or *possession.* He doesn't feel strange and different but well-known and close, as a part of myself.

I think about how it has been, and will be many more times, and I can hardly believe that it happens and that it's I who get to experience it.

I open the cupboard and take out the coffee jar.

When I turn around, he is standing close behind me. He takes the jar out of my hand and places it on the bench without looking at it. He is just looking at me.

He takes me in his arms and holds me close to him. I lean my head against his shoulder and put my arms around his waist and just stand there and feel his warm body against mine.

He takes my head between his hands and kisses me tenderly and gently on my mouth and eyelids.

He looks at me the entire time while he undoes the button at the waist and pulls his shirt out of his jeans. My body is getting ready, and I can hardly breathe. Then he comes up to me and embraces me so gently and excitingly that I get totally weak.

He pulls me up on top of him. I kneel over him, and his hands on my hips press me down. I lean over his face, and he gently pulls his lips over my breasts. The next moment he moans and turns me in a single sweeping motion down on my back.

His arms harden and he looks at me with a steady gaze, so that I understand that he really wants me and that it's just me, and only me, he wants.

He gets up on his knees and takes support with his

hands at my shoulders. I part my legs and receive him, and he comes into me and is in the quiet, warm, darkness where I know he is meant to be. I feel the closeness and the warmth and the quiet togetherness that has no words. I enjoy having him inside me and want him to be there forever.

He is asleep, and I lie enclosed by his arms and feel him with my whole body. I feel his chest and hard stomach and legs. When I move a little, he moves after me in his sleep and holds me even closer to him.

Göran has told his parents and brothers about me. I don't know what he has said, but everyone in his family knows about me now. Göran's two best friends, whom I haven't met yet, also know. And we have told Egon and Viola that we are together. Viola had understood it a long time ago, she said. I don't know how Egon reacted, because he didn't comment on it.

It feels a little insecure that it isn't just Göran and I anymore, as if others can come and interfere and perhaps ruin it. But mamma is the only one who can ruin things, and I am not going to tell her.

If Göran and I move in together, we can sell our apartments and buy a new one together. I didn't think that far before.

But why do we have to live together? I don't want us to share everything. I don't want him to become too familiar to me, so that I might get tired of him. And we are not going to have more interrogations. I don't want to know everything about him, and I don't want him to know everything about me. Every time we have talked a lot, I feel empty and want to withdraw afterwards. I need to be separated from him to regain my longing for him, and how could I do that if we lived together?

Why does my longing sometimes disappear when it's so strong for the most part?

He hasn't suggested that we move together, but what would I say if he brought it up? Would he understand why I don't want it if I explained?

Or is it wrong to say no? Am I just afraid? But why am I afraid? Moving together wouldn't make much difference to how we already have it. Why do I think it would be worse if we only had one apartment?

I get sad when I think about it. I want him and want to be with him and want to love him! If he asks, I must say yes, because that's the right thing to do, and that's truth.

As soon as I get afraid, I start to doubt, and as soon as I start to doubt I lose myself. I have done it many times, and I don't want it to be that way anymore.

Mamma will never get to see him. *He loves me, and you don't! You'll never get to see him! When we move together, you won't get to know where we live! When we get married, you won't be invited to the wedding! I love him and he loves me, and you'll never get to know!*

I don't understand. What has mamma to do with this? Is it her fault that I get scared and doubt? Yes, it's she who has made me weak and unsure of myself. She has to go. She must not ruin it for us. Next time she calls, I will hang up as soon as I hear her voice. I am not going to listen to her or talk to her anymore. There is no other way. I am not strong enough to see her without being affected by how she is and what she does. I must stay out of her reach, so that she doesn't get a grip on me again.

If I imagine that mamma and Göran met, I know he would be able to handle her and not let himself be used. He would be polite and correct, as he is towards customers at work, and he wouldn't make an effort to listen to her if he wasn't interested in what she had to say. She would immediately notice that he wouldn't let her control him, and no matter how good-looking and nice she found him, she would lose interest in him. At first, she might be ingratiating and try to snare him that way, but when that didn't work either, she would give up and dismiss him.

But she will never get to see him. She hasn't deserved it. I will tell him how I have felt about her and how I feel now, and then I don't want to have anything more to do with her.

Göran has also had problems with his parents, and he has told me about it. He already knows, and already does, what I have learned after the rape. He understands that you must free yourself from the past to strengthen yourself so that you can live your life as you want.

He noticed that I understood what he was talking about, and that I agree that this is the way to
go. We felt equal, and we haven't always done so.
It's not his fault. He has never set up any obstacles
for me to reach him. It's with me that obstacles
have existed, when I have become afraid and
doubted. But I have begun to learn how to think
and act when I notice that it happens, so that I can
get past it. I don't want him to be disappointed in
me, when I have never had to be disappointed in
him.

I have been afraid that mental closeness would
reduce the need for bodily closeness, but that's not
how it is. The desire disappears only when I stop
listening to myself and deny the truth.

– Yes, now you know why I don't want to meet her.

– Mm.

*– Didn't you have any problems at all with your par-
ents?*

*– Oh yes. For example, I often felt very unfairly
treated in relation to my brothers.*

– In what way?

*– Both are older than me, and when I wanted to be
together with them and play and they didn't let me, my
mother said I could play with Jenny instead, which in
practice meant that I had to look after her, and I didn't
want to do that. And when my brothers put the blame
on me for various faults, I was never helped by mother
or father to get the truth out, but everything was just*

dismissed as if it was totally unimportant who had done what. But I, who was blamed for things I hadn't done, of course didn't think so. Alone with mother or father in other situations, I was perhaps listened to, but never when it came to quarrels between us children, which both mother and father refused to get involved in and help sort out.

– How did you react to it?

– I tried to protest, but when it didn't help, I learned to keep it to myself and took the anger and frustration out on other people and other things instead. On Jenny, for example, even though she was so little, and of course I felt guilty about that.

– Mm.

– When I got older and it worked better with my brothers, I pretty much forgot everything. But I always reacted very strongly to injustices in various situations. It wasn't until I was reported to the police that time, that I started to think a little more about it, because then I thought I overreacted. Actually, I was totally cracked. And one day, when the feeling was at its strongest, I came to think of what it had been like when I was little and got out of me some of the anger, powerlessness, and sadness that I held back at that time.

– Mm.

– It was a great relief to feel it and understand how it was connected. At the same time, I understood my previous exaggerated reactions to other injustices that I felt I had suffered. So now I try to pay attention to myself when I react stronger than I think is justified. I ask my-

self if it may be a feeling from my childhood that has been aroused. And so it often turns out to be. Much of what I felt after Jenny's death also came from my childhood.

– Mm.

– In the beginning, I was ashamed of focusing on myself. I felt self-absorbed and egoistic. But now I understand that it is my duty to myself, and to others as well, to find out how things are connected. Without self-knowledge, it will only be misunderstanding and hassle.

– Yes, it will.

– Do you know that it's largely taboo to talk about this?

– But it's true. It is the truth.

– Then it is the truth that's taboo.

– What has happened when you have tried?

– That I have encountered closed doors and been called nutcase and pundit and wiseacre.

– Because you have told people how to do it?

– Yes.

– Who did that?

– My brothers, among others.

– Did you want to help them?

– Yes, but it was just stupid. Finally, I realized that I wanted it most for my own sake, so that I could at last be together with them and feel close and in touch. What I wanted and needed when I was little, that is. But now I can do without it.

– Mm.

– Now I realize that I can't do a bit to hurry their

personal development and that it isn't up to me to take responsibility for it either.

– No, that's how I think about mother as well. I understand that she needs help, but if she doesn't want to help herself, it isn't possible. But without the truth, you won't get anywhere.

– No, you won't.

– Without the truth, we wouldn't be lying here now.

– No, we wouldn't. And I couldn't do… like this.

He lies on top of me and kisses me. After a while, he comes into me, and he is there in full. Deep in the warm, wet darkness he is, and I am filled with him to body and soul.

PART EIGHT

Last year before Christmas, when I was sick and I for the first time experienced all the emotions I had during the rape, I thought I would feel stronger afterwards. And I did. I do. But now it's like I have to be aware all the time and must not escape at all. It's as if nothing but the truth is allowed to prevail.

I wasn't afraid when it happened, and I wasn't afraid afterwards, but now I feel afraid sometimes. I feel unprotected and vulnerable. It's only when Göran lies on top of me or behind me and is inside me that I feel really safe, because then no one else can come and take me. I know it's silly, but that's how I experience it. I, who previously found it nice to live alone and wanted to keep him at a distance, no longer want it that way at all. Now I want to see, hear, and be close to him all the time.

And I must be able to bear all my feelings for him and not push them away. It's strenuous. It's easier to be closed and not feel so much. But that's not right.

He is helping me. If I am tired or in a bad mood, he takes me in his arms and lets me feel what I feel and be who I am, and after a while it subsides, and I calm down. And in the warmth, the closeness, and the calm, the physical desire awakens, and I want him even closer to me. Then he is there and meets me and takes over and gives me what I want, which is the same as he wants himself. It's always mutual and in common. He is created to give, and I am created to receive.

Bernt didn't have a chance, and it was my fault. I understand that now. I didn't want him. It wasn't him I wanted. I couldn't open and receive him, but I let him come anyway, and that wasn't right. I should have been honest with him and said no. I should never have been together with him, because I didn't love him. I have nothing to accuse him of. It was all my fault.

But I love Göran. If he left me and we never met again, I would feel like I do for him all the same, and I will do so for as long as I live. What I feel is so deep that it can't be ruined or vanish by external circumstances. Or would it disappear if it wasn't mutual anymore and we never met again?

We don't hold interrogations anymore, but some days we still talk a lot. It's only together with others we are quiet and withdrawn. Our talk can be about anything. Sometimes we drift on to the rape again.

– Do you know what Viola once said?

– No?

– She said that the sexiest thing she knows is a strong man who uses his physical and mental strength to help and protect weak and vulnerable people and animals.

– Yes, that sounds good. That's probably why she is married to a fireman. He has saved the lives of both humans and animals, I've heard.

– Yes, I know. Would you dare to intervene if you saw a girl being assaulted by a man in a dark park?

– Yes, I would.

– How can you be so sure of that?

– Because I wouldn't bear to know that I hadn't tried to help her.

– So, if you had seen when I was assaulted, you would have come and tried to rescue me?

– Yes, I would.

– But he was so big… You wouldn't have been able to overpower him.

– The most likely is that he would be interrupted and run away.

– Do you think so?

– Yes, that's how it usually is.

– How do you know?

– That's what it usually says in the newspapers, and that's how I heard my mother tell it. A rapist doesn't stay and start fighting if he is caught red-handed. There may be exceptions, but the most common is that he runs away.

– Mm.

– Did you call for help?

– Yes. I screamed once, but no one heard or cared about it. "If you scream one more time, I'll kill you", he said. If I had known for sure that people went by out on the street, I would have tried, but it was in the middle of the night and almost no one out. I didn't think he would kill me if I screamed, but he probably would have beaten me.

– Mm. Do you think a lot about what happened?

– No, not anymore. But sometimes I get a feeling of sadness, which may have to do with the rape. I will probably never be really free from it. I don't know. Now afterwards, I think it was fortunate that I was so closed to myself even before it happened, so that it didn't just go straight into me. Otherwise, I would probably have gone crazy.

– Mm.

– It was all so lonely. I got no help. No one came rushing and forcibly heaved him away from me, and no one took care of me and calmed me afterwards. In the police car and at the police station, I had to stay up on my own. And I had no one to tell at home, and later there was no one who could listen when I needed to talk about it or give me support during the trial. I had to cope as best I could, and later I was alone trying to sort it all out.

– You know I would have…

– Yes, I know. But I didn't tell you. You asked, but I rejected you.

– I should have persisted.

– No, it was I who should have asked for help. I do it now sometimes, soundlessly to myself when I'm sad. But at that time, I didn't. Once when you asked, I was close to taking courage and telling you everything. But I stopped myself at the last minute. It wasn't your fault. It was me who couldn't. And then I helped myself, and it was no longer needed. But I still get the feeling sometimes that I need help. It has probably to do with my childhood as well.

– Mm.

– Do you have any feelings that come back to you like that? That can just show up at any time?

– Yes, I have. One is "I can't handle this", and another is "I'm sorry". I ask Jenny for forgiveness both for what I did to her when she was little and when she died.

– And the first feeling also has to do with the accident?

– Yes, it has.

– It's so sad…

– Mm.

– You're sad.

– Yes, it isn't always enough to intervene and try to save.

How much does he understand? I can't expect him to understand what it really was like for me. How could he? I don't understand what it was like for him when his sister died. But when I tell, he listens without defending himself, and knowing that he knows gives me a sense of security and… *anchorage.* Everything he knows about me, and everything I know about him, unites us. It becomes a union where no one else has a part.

I am afraid I have become too dependent on him. I may want greater closeness than it's right to have and may give him too little space, so he feels suffocated. One evening we fell out, and it was my fault. I regretted it almost at once and thought I had overreacted. But it was good that it happened so that I can be sure that he defends himself and isn't too kind if I do wrong to him.

Bernt and I never quarrelled. I thought it was because we had almost the same opinion about everything, but now I understand that it was because the inner distance between us was too great. We didn't care about each other's opinions and feelings enough for any conflicts to arise.

That's not the case with Göran and me. When we disagreed, it started with him saying "that conclusion must be drawn", and it made me remember the time when Bernt started masturbating on the bed beside me and I thought that he "took the thing in his own hands and drew the conclusion himself".

– How many girls have you slept with during your life?

– During my life?

– Yes, be serious now. Altogether, I mean.

– Eight.

– There weren't many for a guy as handsome as you, Viola would say.

– Has Viola said she thinks I'm handsome?

– Yes, don't get cocky now! Why haven't there been more than eight?

– I haven't been so anxious, I guess.

– Why not?

– I want it to be more than just sex. It doesn't feel so good afterwards if it has only been a mutual sexual exploitation.

– No. Have you been done out of it sometime, then?

– Done out of it? Yes, once, when all signs indicated the exact opposite, it was stopped at the last minute.

– What did you do then?

– Interrupted, of course.

– Not everyone would have done that.

– No, but that a guy can't control himself and hold back when the foreplay has reached a certain point is just bullshit. It isn't harder for a guy than for a girl to interrupt.

– Why are there so many guys who don't do it, then?

– Well, who knows? Because they haven't learned to appreciate closeness, warmth, and mutuality and think that the ejaculation is the only important thing? That they haven't learned to show consideration and respect? That they have lacked positive male role models while *growing up? That they have a distorted view of women? That they are influenced by porn and have learned that a man must be macho? A boy in his teens should be interested in sports, motoring, alcohol, and sex. If he isn't, he irretrievably ends up outside. I still remember the talk about girls that my classmates had "fucked", "screwed", and "banged". I never participated in it, but I couldn't avoid hearing. That one has a need at that age to brag and assert oneself isn't so strange, but many don't seem to grow out of it but carry with them the same immature attitude towards women later in life as well.*

– Mm. Why didn't you participate? Why didn't you fall for the peer pressure?

– Partly because I had other interests, but also because I was used to ending up outside and wasn't afraid of it. I think I realized quite early that there are also some benefits to not belonging to a group. And in high school, I had a couple of friends who had the same attitude as I had.

– What do you think about rape?

– Yes, what do I think? That it's incomprehensible how a guy can use his superior physical strength against a defenceless girl to obtain sex by force. Or how he can use his sexual organ as a… hostile weapon, when in fact it's quite the opposite. What harm doesn't that do to the guy himself? But he is probably already damaged, one must assume, because otherwise he wouldn't be able to behave like that. He doesn't feel more respect for himself than he does for the girl.

– What can you do about it, then?

– On the whole, you mean?

– Yes.

– I don't know… Stricter laws, harsher penalties, longer so-called care? I don't know how far one would come with that. The goal is to get men to stop raping, and I think that's as difficult as getting men to stop drinking or fighting.

– Yes, because all of it is actually an escape from pain.

– Yes, and to free yourself from mental pain you can only do yourself and not force others to do.

– Yes, that's the way it is.

– The two members of the wiseacre club express themselves!

– But it's true.

– Yes, but not many people want to recognize that truth. Already old Jung was of the opinion that self-insight is crucial for whether we should be able to do good in society and achieve peaceful solutions in a larger perspective. He hoped and believed it would be the goal of all human beings to increase the goodness and justice of the world. The more people come into contact with their inner truth, the greater the hope for a bright future for our earth, he said. And that's naturally true. But how do you make self-knowledge the "goal of all human beings"? He was probably a little too naive and optimistic, our friend Jung.

– Yes, it hasn't happened yet anyway. I don't think people are motivated enough. If not even seemingly normal persons, like my mother and your brothers, don't

feel motivated, then how could rapists and murderers do it?

– No, it isn't very likely.

– Hopeless, then.

– Yes, you can probably draw that conclusion.

– Mm. Have you masturbated a lot during your life?

– Now I don't follow you… Masturbated? What has that to do with…

– Just answer the question.

– The interrogator exerts pressure?

– Yes, no evasions now!

– Yes, I probably have.

– Promise that you'll never do it so I can see it.

– Why don't you want to see it?

– I think it's embarrassing. It looks silly and unworthy. Pathetic.

– Who have you seen doing it?

– Bernt.

– No one else?

– No.

– Okay. When a girl does it, then?

– I don't want to see that either.

– When you do it yourself, then?

– Then I don't see it from the outside, so it's not the same. I forgot to say, when I told you about the rape before, that while we were still standing up and he was pushing me against the wall, I tried to masturbate him so that he might let me go. At that time, I didn't know that rape has more to do with power than with sex.

– When you were in the yard?

– Yes. I grabbed it and held it in my hand. But it didn't work. I just helped him to get an erection. That was kind of me, wasn't it? To make him physically capable of raping me, I mean.

– Is that why you...

– No, it has nothing to do with him. He didn't do it himself. It's only when the guy does it himself that I find it embarrassing.

– Okay.

– What are you thinking about?

– You have told me quite a lot about your mother but almost nothing about your father.

– No, I just dismissed him. I didn't think I needed to care about him. But I did. Every time he showed that he didn't understand my needs... I have been angry and sorry about that. But that may not be all. There is perhaps more... Yes, now I understand what you think. But that's not how it is. It's not from papa I've got it. I'm pretty sure of that. He was just uninterested and absent.

– Okay.

– Do you think it's strange that I don't like to see it?

– I don't know.

– I wouldn't want you to see me do it on myself either.

– No?

– No, I think masturbation is a private matter.

– Yes, it is.

– If I masturbate, it's because I'm alone and you aren't here. If I were to do it in your presence, it would feel like I was deselecting you. Like I would rather be *aroused by what I myself thought and did than by you. So, I can't do it. I can't. Then sex would only be sex. And you said you want it to be more?*

– And inversely, you would feel disregarded? If I started touching myself instead of you?

– Yes, I would. Then I might as well go away. Then I'm not needed.

– You would react as if I were unfaithful to you with myself.

– Yes, that's how it would feel.

– Well, I haven't thought much about it, but I may have had the idea that the private things one showed would increase intimacy and not decrease it.

– Yes, but that wouldn't work for me. It's you and not just a sexual organ and an orgasm I want!

– Yes, okay.

– Sorry. I don't know why I'm so upset.

– Because you're disappointed in me?

– Yes, I don't want it to be the case that some fine day we have to tinker and get up to tricks with our bodies to be able to have sex! Mechanical sex I got enough of with Bernt. But if that's how you want it so…

– No, that's not how I want it! I just haven't thought about it.

– Do it now then and let me know.

– But for Christ's sake! I understand what you mean! I know what we have! I know what is true!

– Yes, because I haven't struggled to dare to believe in this just because you would come and say later that it isn't worth much! When it's not you I want anymore

but just your body, it's over!

– I had better behave then, so that you don't get tired of me.

– No, I didn't mean… Sorry I got angry. Sorry! Of course, you have the right to do as you please. If I don't want to see, I can just go away. But now I at least know that you can get angry.

– Yes, of course I can get angry! Didn't you think so?

– I've never seen you angry.

– Now you have.

– Yes, and I know I shouldn't have said it like I did.

When I realized how wrong I had done him, I regretted it and began to cry. I cried and apologized. It felt like I had committed a great sin, and the feeling of guilt overwhelmed me.

He didn't say anything. He understood that it was best that he was quiet. He understood that he shouldn't touch me. And when I got up and went into the bedroom, he understood that he would come after me and lie down next to me on the bed and comfort me with his body. I lay in his arms and cried against his chest and said I was sorry.

– No, I'm the one to ask for forgiveness. You shouldn't have any vague ideas that you haven't questioned and gone to the bottom with.

– But it can also have to do with my mamma, that I can't stand that someone only deals with his own needs and ignores me. Maybe that's why I reacted so strongly.

– Yes, it can be.

– It may not have been so fun for you either, when I was closed and couldn't be reached. When you tried and I just rejected you.

– I should have tried harder.

– No, it was good that I got to do it at my own pace. That it was my need and not yours that drove me.

It ended as it always does, and when it happened this time, I knew everything was okay again. As soon as I felt the desire coming, I knew it. Otherwise, it wouldn't have come. The body never lies. The brain can lie sometimes but not the body.

To do wrong to him is much worse than to do wrong to myself. But if I make a mistake against myself, it also affects him. It's indistinguishable.

He gives me understanding, respect, tenderness, comfort, and pleasure, and I want to give the same to him. I want it to be fair. According to Petra, there is no equality between the sexes. Not out in the community and not in a close relationship. But inequality exists between people of the same sex as well.

And I think that Göran and I are equal. When it comes to practical things, we try to divide, help, and be fair. Emotionally, it's also fair. As soon as an imbalance arises, I try to correct it. When I feel that I receive more than I give, I feel uncomfortable because I know what it is like to be the one who only gives. I don't want him to feel that way about me. I want it to be mutual. It has to be, because otherwise it won't work.

When I was new at the office, it was Viola who took care of me and put me to work. By then, Göran had already been there for two years.

It's Egon who owns the accounting firm, but I haven't much to do with him during a normal working day. It's Viola I meet the most. We sit in the same room and have the same kind of work tasks, so we talk quite a lot. She isn't at all like mamma, that she does all the talking herself the entire time, but she also listens, so it works well to cooperate with her. I don't feel very confident in her, and I don't tell her any personal matters, but she does tell me sometimes, and she always declares what she thinks about things. To Egon too, if she finds him behaving inappropriately or is expressing a worthless opinion.

Once when she saw him touching me, she told him off properly. He had given me a pat on the behind, and to me it was the same kind of pat that papa used to give me when he was tired of me and told me to run out and play. When Viola reacted as if what Egon was doing had a sexual meaning,

I felt stupid for not understanding it. I felt that he treated me condescendingly at times, but I thought his touches were just a way for him to be kind to me. I didn't understand that it had to do with sex for his part.

Now I avoid getting close to him so as not to give him a chance to touch me. If he succeeded, I don't really know how I would react. I am not sure I would feel offended enough to speak out. He is just a boring old man who I don't have to pay any attention to and who you can almost feel sorry for.

It's not good to be indulgent with people who are not able to do the right thing. I know that. But I avoid and ignore rather than protest and reprimand a person who feels totally insignificant to me. It's not out of cowardice I do it, but out of indifference.

I don't know if Göran has noticed Egon's behaviour towards me. He should have done it, but he has never commented on it. He knows I can handle it myself and doesn't interfere.

When we are at work, I feel that we are enclosed in a dark tunnel that no one else can enter. That's where we meet. Outside the tunnel it's grey and dull. Not unpleasant or painful, but empty and indifferent. Being in the office all day and performing tedious tasks almost feels like betraying and abandoning oneself. It doesn't give me anything. It may never have done it, although I haven't realized it. Previously, I had nothing that meant more.

But now I feel that I may have to start studying and training for a profession that suits me better.

Every day after dinner when we have cleared the table, we lay down on the bed and let our thoughts come and go. We don't talk, as we do while we eat, but we are both in our own minds while our bodies are close together. I get calm and relaxed doing so, and so does he, he says.

He lies behind me with his arms around me and protects me from all evil. Sometimes when I have thought or done wrong and got away from the truth, I cry and feel: *I love you, I love you, I love you!* I feel it, but I don't say it. I have never told him that I love him, and he has never said that he loves me. The words would diminish and limit what we have, and we don't want that to happen. At least, that's how I interpret it.

Sometimes when I sleep restlessly and perhaps have a nightmare, he holds me and whispers: "It's okay, I'm here." Then I cry because he does so and because no one did so when I was little and needed it.

It hurts that he loves me. Previously, I felt both sorrow and pain, but now it's mostly pain. He is the one who causes it, and only he can alleviate it. I understand that it isn't right to want to meet only one person, and that it's wrong to use him as pain relief. But that's how I feel, and that's what I do. I hide it from him and hope it will pass over. But I am afraid. What if I never get stronger than this and ruin everything we have?

I still get physically aroused by him and I still want him inside me, but now it's more difficult for me to come. Is it because I have become too dependent on him and can no longer manage myself? Am I about to change into a helpless baby who needs physical contact to not die?

Didn't mamma take good care of me when I was new-born? Did she leave me crying and alone in bed? Didn't I get food when I was hungry? Didn't she give me physical closeness and comfort? Is that why the pain exists? Is that why I need Göran more than I should?

I must not do that to him. I want to love him for his own sake, for who he is, and not for what he can give me. I must differentiate then and now. What I didn't get when I was little, it isn't up to him to give me. If he evokes feelings that belong to my childhood, I must be strong and endure the pain and don't try to run away. I must not use him to escape. I must resist it and get through it.

– Do you think we withdraw from other people and keep too much to ourselves?

– What do you mean?

– Well, that we don't meet so many others.

– But we do, don't we? I meet Patrik and Andreas and you meet Petra.

– Yes, but it's been a long time since you met your family.

– I didn't do it often before I met you either.

– Don't you miss them?

– No, I don't. We are calling. That's enough for me. I have no need for superficial company.

– Superficial?

– Yes, at family gatherings and family reunions, not much of interest is said.

– It's not me who hinders you then, from meeting others and doing other things than just being with me?

– No, you're not hindering me. Do you think so?

– No, I'm just asking. Do you think we should be more alone, each one of us, then?

– No, I don't. To be alone, we are free to be whenever we want, aren't we?

– Yes, I'm just asking.

– Why? Why do you ask?

– Because I've heard that it isn't good for a love couple to withdraw from others and be together too much.

– Why isn't it good?

– If you don't get stimulation from outside, or aren't just by yourself sometimes, you eventually have nothing to bring into the relationship, and then it fades away and dies.

– The relationship dies?

– Yes.

– Do you feel there is a risk of that?

– No, not for us. I'm just saying what I've heard. And I can't know for sure how you feel.

– Yes, you can.

– But it's just the two of us. We have almost no friends, no deep relationships with others, no need to meet others. The majority want company and fellowship, want to belong to a group and socialize, but we just withdraw and keep to ourselves. Maybe it's a stingy and selfish way of living? Maybe it isn't normal?

– No, it probably isn't, if you with normal mean what the majority does. In that case, I have never been quite normal.

– Neither have I. You don't think it's wrong, then? Not being outgoing and social, I mean, and not being interested in trying to help others?

– No, I don't think so. You must do what suits you best.

– Yes, because I can't. I don't want to. I have tried to be lenient and understanding, but I have only lost by that. It has only led to it becoming bad for myself. And I don't want it that way any longer.

– Good.

– I feel lousy and disobliging, but let people think I am then, because I can't anymore! I have the right to be honest and show how I feel.

– Yes, you have.

– I don't want to pretend and put it on.

– No, you don't have to.

– But it's like I can't overlook the smallest little thing anymore.

– Like what?

– Like that the aunt who lives above me snapped   at me even though I had only asked a friendly question. She has talked to me in the elevator and in the laundry room and asked how grandpa is doing and so on, and I have asked her about things too, and then she has always been kind and nice. But now it was as if she suddenly thought I was awkward, and after that it feels like I have distanced myself from her and can't even bring myself to say hallo to her. It's as if the TRUTH has come out. She doesn't like me, and I don't like her. That's the truth. You MUST actually pretend and put it on when you meet people who you aren't very familiar with. The mistake I made was that I hadn't made it clear to myself that I don't like her. Now that I know, I can probably be false and say hallo. But I don't have to feel and show confidence in her, as I did before. I can be as false to her as I am to some unsympathetic customers at work.

– Mm.

– Another question then: Do you think we idealize each other?

– Idealize? No, why would we do that?

– Because that's what you usually do at the beginning of an infatuation. You only see what you want to see and always show yourself from your best side.

– Not so much reality, that is?

– Yes.

– When will reality begin to appear, then?

– When the passion is over, and you have moved together.

– Okay.

– Say some things about me that annoy you.

– Annoy me? Well, let's see… First, we have this that you always have to… You need to be prepared that the list may be long.

– Yes, it's okay.

– No, I'm just joking! There's nothing about you that annoys me. What is it about me that annoys you, then?

– Nothing.

– Then we are obviously still in the blind phase of passion.

– Yes, or we are both absolutely perfect.

– Yes, that's probably how it is. We have no faults and shortcomings at all!

– Have you never done any stupid things?

– Yes, of course I have.

– Like what?

– What most people try when they are young. I have pilfered and smoked and got drunk and cycled without a light… How about you?

– I have smoked, as you know, and I did it for seven years. That's probably the stupidest thing I have done, if I don't count in that I was together with Bernt.

– Mm.

– I have another question about what we talked about before.

– Yes?

– Do you think I want too much closeness, so you get

too little space and feel suffocated?

– No, I like closeness. Don't you know that? I don't feel suffocated. I feel free. Why are you asking all this?

– Because I have thought about it, and because Petra and I have been talking about it.

– You have talked about what can kill a relationship?

– Yes, she has been together with quite a few guys and doesn't understand why it never lasts. She wonders what she's doing wrong.

– Okay.

– What did you think of her when she was here?

– I thought she was a lively and energetic type. Out-spoken.

– Do you like that type?

– Yes, but I easily become passive and quiet in their company, as you may have noticed.

– Me too. But what did you think of her?

– Yes, what did I think… That she was entertaining, I guess.

– Bernt didn't like her at all, and it was mutual.

– Mhm.

– I have heard that if a couple likes each other's friends, it strengthens their relationship.

– Now we are on the relationship again.

– Yes.

– Do you worry about how your and my relationship will go?

– No, I don't. But sometimes I'm afraid I'm going to make a mistake.

– There must be room for that.

– Yes, and I know there is. It's not you I'm unsure of. It's of myself.

– In what way?

– That I have too poor self-knowledge, so I don't always do the right thing and maybe complicate things unnecessarily. It's just that.

– It's the same for me. But that's nothing to worry about. If there is a problem, we'll sort it out. To help each other, and solve problems together, also have a strengthening effect on the relationship, I've heard.

– Mm.

– And this, I notice… also has a certain… effect.

His voice, his hands, his eyes, his body.

His soul in the dark tunnel.

PART NINE

The sorrow is gone. The pain appears sometimes, but not as often as before. I have cried and called for mamma and asked her to come and take care of me, but she hasn't come. *She didn't come,* and it felt like I was going to die.

Now that I know what it really was like and I have given up hope on her, I can meet her without being sad or losing myself. I can handle it and I am not angry with her anymore. But that doesn't mean I *want to* meet her. I don't want it, and I don't do it. I don't care about her and don't want to see her. I care about her as little as she cares about me and don't let myself be used. I can say no and don't try to dodge out of it.

It's the same with Egon, that I feel clearly where the limit goes, and I am prepared to protest if he should try to exceed it. I am not on my guard against him anymore, because it stands to reason that I should be able to move freely at work without having to be molested.

I have been so credulous and stupid. I won't be that anymore. I regret that I have thought well of everybody for no reason at all. I regret that I have been open and accommodating and hoped for understanding and respect from people who haven't been worth showing myself to.

I regret it. And the fact that I feel my own worth now, and know what is right for me, means that I have lost interest in studying psychology. I understand how difficult it would be to help others to find themselves, and I don't want to deal with it. I have helped myself and I can't bear more than that. Not yet anyway. I am tired of other people's problems and just want to be with Göran and myself.

All evenings, all nights, and all days off, we are together, and I never get enough. It's not just sex. It's also another kind of pleasure, which he gives me just by looking at me, taking me in his arms, or lying beside me in bed and sleeping. I feel cherished, grateful, and secure.

Imagine if I had never got to experience it.

Imagine if I had never got to feel comfort and pleasure.

To the very last, he has been waiting for me. He loves me and I love him. But as long as I used him for protection, comfort and pain relief, I couldn't say that I love him, because then it wasn't entirely true. Now it is. And when I for the first time told him, he was there. I lay in his arms and said it against his chest.

– I love you.

– Aha.

– Yes. And you love me.

– Yes, I do. I love you.

– And that's all.

– Yes, that's all.

He has been here all along and received me. He isn't aware of it anymore. I feel that. He isn't in control. It's his love for me, and my love for him, that prevails, and it's greater than both his and my awareness. We are not the ones who decide. The only thing we can do is acknowledge the truth and give in to it. And we do, because we have no choice.